Here's what critics are saying about Gemma Halliday's books:

"A saucy combination of romance and suspense that is simply irresistible."
—*Chicago Tribune*

"Stylish...nonstop action...guaranteed to keep chick lit and mystery fans happy!"
—*Publishers' Weekly*, starred review

"Smart, funny and snappy…the perfect beach read!"
—*Fresh Fiction*

"A roller coaster ride full of fun and excitement!"
—*Romance Reviews Today*

"Gemma Halliday writes like a seasoned author leaving the reader hanging on to every word, every clue, every delicious scene of the book. It's a fun and intriguing mystery full of laughs and suspense."
—*Once Upon A Romance*

BOOKS BY GEMMA HALLIDAY

High Heels Mysteries
Spying in High Heels
Killer in High Heels
Undercover in High Heels
Christmas in High Heels (short story)
Alibi in High Heels
Mayhem in High Heels
Honeymoon in High Heels (short story)
Sweetheart in High Heels (short story)
Fearless in High Heels
Danger in High Heels
Homicide in High Heels
Deadly in High Heels
Suspect in High Heels
Peril in High Heels
Jeopardy in High Heels

Wine & Dine Mysteries
A Sip Before Dying
Chocolate Covered Death
Victim in the Vineyard
Marriage, Merlot & Murder
Death in Wine Country
Fashion, Rosé & Foul Play
Witness at the Winery

Hollywood Headlines Mysteries
Hollywood Scandals
Hollywood Secrets
Hollywood Confessions
Hollywood Holiday (short story)
Hollywood Deception

Marty Hudson Mysteries
Sherlock Holmes and the Case of the Brash Blonde
Sherlock Holmes and the Case of the Disappearing Diva
Sherlock Holmes and the Case of the Wealthy Widow

Tahoe Tessie Mysteries
Luck Be A Lady
Hey Big Spender
Baby It's Cold Outside (holiday short story)

Jamie Bond Mysteries
Unbreakable Bond
Secret Bond
Bond Bombshell (short story)
Lethal Bond
Dangerous Bond
Bond Ambition (short story)
Fatal Bond
Deadly Bond

Hartley Grace Featherstone Mysteries
Deadly Cool
Social Suicide
Wicked Games

Other Works
Play Dead
Viva Las Vegas
A High Heels Haunting
Watching You (short story)
Confessions of a Bombshell Bandit (short story)

A SIP BEFORE DYING

---

a Wine & Dine mystery

GEMMA HALLIDAY

Dedicated to the memory of Amy Louise.

CHAPTER ONE

My best friend was waiting for me outside Silver Girl, her jewelry boutique in downtown Sonoma, when I pulled up in my Jeep. Ava Barnett: blonde, bubbly, and as perpetually optimistic as a woman who worked the tourist trade could be. She was dressed today in a flowy floral dress that just skirted her perfectly tanned ankles above boho-style sandals and pink painted toenails. We were both about a size eight, though Ava was on the lithe, athletic side of eight, and I was on the generous, enjoys-her-chocolate side of eight. She floated into my passenger seat on a cloud of peachy lotion and patchouli incense, and I instantly felt my spirits lift as I tried to downplay how rotten that Friday had turned out for me.

"How's things?" she asked, chucking her overnight bag into the back seat of the Wrangler.

I shrugged, tucking some of my flyaways back into my ponytail. While Ava's hair shone, humidity or cloudless sky, my own blonde locks were a fickle bunch. I had my good days, but depending on the weather, they could kink up like Shirley Temple or frizz like Bozo the Clown. Today they were somewhere at a half-Bozo, hence the ponytail to rein them in. "Things are fine," I answered, determined to put on a happy face.

She grinned at me, showing off a row of white teeth with an endearingly chic gap between the front two. "Liar."

I couldn't help the corners of my mouth turning up as well. Joined at the hip since high school, we were more like sisters than best friends. Ava knew me well enough to see through any attempt at downplay.

"Okay, honestly? Things kinda sucked today," I told her.

"Really?" Her big brown eyes turned sympathetic.

I nodded. "Like a Hoover."

"Is it your mom?" she asked.

I bit my lip, feeling a whole new wave of suckatude wash over me at the mention of my mother. But I shut off that emotional faucet before it could completely ruin our planned girls' night. I shook my head. "No, today it was Gene. He was pulling his seesaw act again."

Ava had already heard on multiple occasions how Gene Schulz, my financial consultant, played seesaw with his left and right hands, swinging them up and down alternately as he pictured my winery's financial health. The left hand represented debt, and it always ended up at the highest point when the seesaw gesture stopped. Today's game had ended with the right hand falling even lower than in the past. That was the hand that represented assets—in other words, Oak Valley Vineyard and everything I held dear in this world. All I had inherited after my father passed and Mom's beautiful personality had begun to disintegrate.

The assets in question amounted to just over ten acres of vines and a majestic oak-lined driveway that led to a cluster of low Spanish-style buildings that comprised our winery, my own small cottage, and "the cave," as my namesake, Grandma Emmeline, used to call the wine cellar. Down there in the cool dark was my barreled and bottled stock in trade: Pinot Noir, Chardonnay, Pinot Blanc, Zinfandel, and a few cases of a small run Petite Sirah.

According to Gene, the whole shebang was worth about half a million dollars less than the outstanding debt. We were hanging on by a fraying thread, and I knew only too well that a couple of sexy big commercial wineries were hovering like vultures, waiting to get Oak Valley Vineyard for a song when it went belly-up. Which they fully expected it to do.

Truth be told, sometimes I thought Gene did too.

In my darkest moments after my mom's diagnosis, I'll admit, I had half expected that as well. While I'd excelled at culinary school and spent several years as a personal chef in Los Angeles, the knowledge I had about running a winery could fit in a fortune cookie. Like generations before me, I'd grown up on the land and had a fair understanding of the crops. But I'd been a teenager when I'd left to strike out my own path. Little did I know that at age twenty-nine, that path would end up leading me right back to Sonoma—only now it was up to me to preserve what my family had worked so hard for.

And as long as I was at the helm, belly-up was not an option.

"So what did Seesaw Gene have to say?" Ava asked.

"He said we'll be lucky to break even this year." I tried to keep my eyes on the road as I pulled out. "We're servicing the debt, and we've never defaulted, knock on wood"—I rapped my knuckles on the faux wood center console—"but we're just scraping by."

"Hey, you're getting by! That's not a bad thing."

I shot her a grin. What did I tell you—Miss Optimism, right?

"Unfortunately, getting by will only last so long." I paused, digging deep for a little enthusiasm. "So, we need to kick it up a notch."

Ava arched one delicate blonde eyebrow at me. "Which is where I come in?"

I nodded. "This weekend, you are my social wheel greaser, mood lifter, and all around hostess with the mostest." I sent her a sympathetic glance. "Sorry, you'll be run ragged, girl."

If she dreaded it, she didn't show it, just giving me another breezy smile. "What are friends for?"

"Have I mentioned lately how much I love you?"

Ave laughed. "Say it with a bottle of your 2012 Blanc, and I'm yours."

"Done," I promised.

The following day was the first event in my grand plan to revive Oak Valley Vineyard, our unofficial re-launch. My aim was to show the local enthusiasts that, while we put out wine to rival any of the big boys in town, we were also a charming venue for parties, weddings, and retreats. And the food wasn't half bad either.

"So, what's on the agenda tonight?" Ava asked.

"Well, I think we should start with that 2012 bottle."

"I concur!"

"And then I'm thinking it's a *Thelma & Louise* night."

"Wow, we're at T&L level?" Ava patted my shoulder. "Must have been a really bad meeting with Gene."

I nodded. "We're gonna need comfort food too." Friday night was no time to count calories.

Ava raised her eyebrow my way again. "Pizza?"

I laughed. "I was thinking more like bacon wrapped scallops. With bacon Brussels. And chocolate dipped bacon." I did mention I was on the *generous* side of a size 8.

Ava shrugged. "Okay, you're the boss."

"*Tomorrow* I'm the boss," I corrected her. "Tonight all I want is some Geena Davis and a girl's night."

"That," Ava said, "I can do."

CHAPTER TWO

The following morning I was up before dawn, walking Conchita, my house manager, and the three local day servers I'd hired for the event through the finer points of my Spanish Style Paella recipe at an improvised fireplace of loose bricks at the edge of the vineyard.

We had a private tasting slated for that afternoon, after which I'd be serving a Spanish meal, all cooked outdoors on wood fires, like the Valencians of the Orange Blossom Coast did at seaside picnics—or at least that was what I would be telling my guests in order to add a European flair to the evening. I planned to serve the meal family-style, outdoors on rustic-chic wooden tables under the trees, and paired with an ice-cold pitcher of sangria at each table made of our Zinfandel, club soda, a splash of brandy, and a pinch of sugar.

"I think we should prepare all the components of the paella in advance, before final assembly," I mused out loud to Conchita. "Brown the meats and have the *sofrito* bubbling away."

Conchita nodded, her salt-and-pepper hair bobbing up and down in the loose bun at the back of her plump neck. She'd been at the winery as long as I could remember, and I almost thought of her as a second mother. Though, with her envious dark tan and Hispanic heritage, she looked the polar opposite of my blue-eyed, bought-sunscreen-in-bulk self. Conchita was married to Hector Villarreal, our vineyard manager, who'd been a fixture at Oak Valley Vineyard since boyhood. I'd learned a lot about the vines from him growing up, and I'd even been the flower girl when he married Conchita. While some might refer to the couple as staff, to me they were family. Some days they almost felt like all the family I had left.

I ignored that downer, though, as Conchita and I worked side by side, adding a splash of oil to a hot pan, along with a finely chopped mixture of onion and seeded tomato, some sweet peppers, and a hint of crushed garlic and parsley. I seasoned it with salt and pepper and a few threads of fragrant saffron then fried it until the *sofrito*—or fry-up—began to form a paste.

"That smells amazing," Conchita told me.

I nodded. "From your mouth to our guests' ears."

She patted my back. "Don't worry. You know they are going to love this."

Love to eat? Yes. Love enough to book their next big event here? I could only hope.

I left the food in Conchita's capable hands and excused myself to get ready for the VIP guests I'd be meeting that day, including local influencers, bloggers, and reporters, as well as socialites, Silicon Valley billionaires, and wine enthusiasts.

No pressure there.

I showered and threw on my usual minimal-but-tasteful makeup routine. I prayed for a good hair day, as I attempted to de-frizz via copious hair products. Which was at least mildly successful. Then I slid on a flattering navy shift dress and a pair of red pumps with low heels, as a concession to the amount of walking I'd be doing on the grass that afternoon. I capped it off with Grammy Em's pearl drop earrings and stood back to assess my reflection. I took a deep breath, praying I could project confidence and not the bundle of nerves I could feel brewing in my stomach.

Fifteen minutes later, I was standing in the circular drive at the head of the estate, awaiting our first guest. Ava was by my side in a clinging forest green sheath, showing one of her own silver crescent moon pendants above a moderate-to-serious amount of cleavage. She squeezed my hand and gave me a fortifying smile as the sound of the first set of tires crunching up the gravel drive approached.

Vivienne Price-Pennington arrived precisely on time in a big white Rolls Royce. While I'd seen her name in the society pages of our local lifestyle magazine, this was the first time I'd encountered the software billionairess in person. Like many of Silicon Valley's elite, she had a second home here in wine country. The CEO of Price Digital was only a couple of inches taller than my own 5'5", but she seemed to take up a lot of space, her personality radiating from her as she stepped from the vehicle in tailored silk and signature red-soled Louboutins. She had a good fifteen to twenty years on me, and the tight fit of her dress over her hips, the extensions in her dyed auburn hair, and the predatory gleam in her eye all said cougar with a capital *C*. Which she could well afford to be, her first three companies having been bought out by Microsoft, Apple, and Intel.

She was accompanied by a young man with dark hair that fell rebelliously into his eyes as he surveyed the vineyard with a perma-scowl on his features. It was a look I'd seen often on the young, idle, and rich in the Bay Area. Beside him stood an older woman with a pinched smile. She wore her A-line skirt and blazer like a starched uniform, complete with hat and gloves, looking almost like a caricature of a society lady on a weekend picnic.

"Mrs. Price-Pennington," I said, reaching to shake my first VIP's hand. "It's a pleasure to finally meet you."

She nodded, glancing behind me at the winery, as if assessing its worth. "Please, call me Vivienne. And it's a pleasure to be here. I've heard good things about your small run Petite Sirah."

"I'll be sure to set a case aside for you," I promised, knowing full well who she'd heard it from. While Gene "Seesaw" Shultz might have his doubts about our long-term solvency, he knew how to push an investment. He'd supplied many of the names on our guest list of the wine loving elite in Sonoma.

"This is my son, David," Vivienne said, gesturing to the younger man.

He nodded awkwardly, as if just "my son, David" was a label he was well used to wearing. I shook his hand, which was slightly sweaty despite the cool spring air.

"And this is my mother, Alison Price."

Alison gave me a gloved hand that had a surprisingly firm grip. Like her daughter, she was tall, though her hair was a duller brown shot with a generous amount of white. Her face looked naturally lined and Botox-free, though her spine was straight and strong. If I had to guess, I put the baby boomer around seventy, though there was nothing frail looking about the senior citizen.

"How do you do?" she asked, clearly not caring what the answer to that question was as she quickly turned her attention away from me and toward her grandson. "David, please get my bag from the trunk."

His scowl deepened, but he ducked back toward the car to obey.

I quickly introduced Ava to the women and told Vivienne, "Ava's on your table. If you need anything, she'll see to it."

Vivienne nodded. "I'm looking forward to this Spanish theme of yours. I've just been back from Europe, so I'm intrigued to see your take on it."

While it was phrased as a statement, it almost came off as a dare. One I planned to take on, guns blazing. "I'm sure you'll enjoy it." I shot her a smile that I hoped was a lot more confident than I felt.

If she noted any of the nerves coursing through me, she didn't mention them, instead gesturing back down the driveway the way she'd come. "My husband, Chas, was held up at work, so he'll be coming later in the Lamborghini. I'm sure he'll be here in time for the picnic, even if he happens to miss the tasting."

I nodded, mentally making a note to treat anyone arriving in a Lamborghini as Price-Pennington royalty. "We'll be sure to direct him to your table when he arrives."

Ava and I ushered the party into the tasting bar, where my bar manager and wine steward, Jean Luc, was preparing his stand-up enologist act. Though, as I'd learned when I'd hired him on last year, Jean Luc preferred the term *sommelier* to wine steward. In fact, I'd quickly learned that Jean Luc preferred the French term for anything to the English. While pretension practically dripped from his thick accent, customers ate it up with silver spoons, today being no exception as I saw Mrs. Price actually crack a genuine smile as he complimented her flower studded hat. My hired day help poured samples for the other guests, and Jean Luc laid on the charm, talking up the Pinot Noir and Chardonnay we had in glass to Vivienne.

I left Ava in the tasting bar to help Jean Luc and slipped outside to stand at the top end of the avenue and say a mental prayer for success, on the lookout for more cars. One by one they arrived, playing out much as the meeting with Vivienne had. Guests had never been here but were curious to see how the little winery with a growing reputation would pull it off today. The more people who arrived, the more I felt like I was on the job interview of a lifetime. This one meal could make or break our word of mouth.

I wasn't sure if all the guests had arrived, but I had run a rough car count, which came out to at least thirty influential people, all squeezed into the tasting bar, mingling and murmuring amongst themselves. The atmosphere in that little bar was heady, as if the very air had an alcohol content. The wine jargon flowed whenever the crowd of like-minded enthusiasts took a short break from sniffing and sipping. They pulled all the faces you'd expect to see at tastings—pouting and puffing their cheeks, breathing in through the nose over a mouthful of my Chardonnay, squeezed between tongue and palate. They gargled the contents of their glasses and talked about the "robe," the "nose," and the "legs."

I turned and walked back to the kitchen, where Conchita was busy organizing the covered plates of paella components and urging the staff on as they transferred the ingredients to a long table under the trees. Outside, I checked the fires in a line of six improvised brick barbecues. Chicken pieces were browning in the sizzling pans, and the rustic tables were all laid, complete with place cards, flowers, and a central board on each, to bear the heat of the pan.

Back in the tightly packed tasting bar, I asked Ava to keep an eye on the proceedings outside, as I threaded my way through the huddled guests, meeting and greeting. Hector had joined Jean Luc and was fielding questions like a pro. One man I recognized as a reporter for *Sonoma Wine Life* asked if the wine would have any taint from the ash and smoke of the previous year's monster wildfires, which had devastated enormous tracts of northern California.

Hector put the newspaperman's fears to rest by saying, "The wines on offer had gone into bottle long before the fires broke out. As for the crop yet to be harvested, time will tell, ladies and gentlemen. It will take a couple of years before we'll know if there's a taint. Let's cross that bridge when we come to it. Personally, I'm inclined to think that Mother Nature will shrug off the effects of the fires."

The reporter smiled, obviously pleased with the answer, and sipped from his glass. I let a moment of relief rush over me.

A short moment.

Ava appeared at my side and whispered, "More guests just arrived, in a sports car."

"Lamborghini?"

Ava shrugged. "Beats me. All I know is it was bright yellow and flashy, and the driver was positively yummy. If he'd arrived alone, you know I would be talking to him right now and not you." She winked at me.

I grinned back. "Down, girl."

She held her hands up in surrender. "Hey, I'm just saying." She paused, nodding toward the doorway. "That's him."

I had to admit, Ava was right. The man filling the doorframe was hot enough to start his own wildfires. Dark blond hair, just long enough on top to be stylish but short enough on the sides to feel GQ. His skin was tanned, jaw square, shoulders broad. He could have been a male model, complete with the perpetually bored look on his face as he surveyed the crowd.

But it was the short brunette at his side that caught my attention. She wore a simple sundress, low-heeled sandals, and was one of the only women in the room *not* carrying a purse sporting a designer logo. I recognized her instantly, though it had been a good decade since I'd seen her. Jennifer Pacheco had been a couple of years behind me in school, and we'd taken choir together my senior year. I remembered her as a shy, quiet kind of girl, though she'd had the voice of an angel.

"Jenny?" I asked, approaching.

She turned a pair of big blue eyes my way, recognition dawning on her side as well. "Emmy!" She gave me a quick hug. "So good to see you again."

"You too. How have you been?" My eyes must have flitted up to her companion, as she immediately introduced him.

"Oh, Emmy, this is my brother, Chas. Chas Pennington."

I blinked, trying to cover my surprise. Pennington, as in my VIP's husband. The cover model beside Jenny was at best a flirty thirty. Several years Vivienne's junior.

"*Half* brother," Chas corrected Jenny, sticking a hand out toward me. "Charmed."

"Nice to meet you," I said, trying to find the resemblance between the two.

"Is my wife here?" he asked, his eyes going to the crowd again.

"Yes, I, uh, believe she's with my wine steward, Jean Luc." I pointed to the bar.

Chas turned his bored look toward his *half* sister, and his eyes softened. "I'll catch up with you later?"

Jenny nodded. "Go. I know how Vivienne hates you being late."

Chas snorted but gave his sister a quick kiss on the cheek before heading toward my VIP.

"I didn't know you had a brother," I said as I watched him walk away. I had to admit, the rear view of his perfectly fitted slacks was not entirely a terrible one. Vivienne knew how to pick them.

Jenny nodded. "You wouldn't have. He lived with his mom in Fremont when we were in high school, so he wasn't at Sonoma Valley High. Plus, we have different last names, of course."

I nodded. "Did Chas take his mother's name?"

Jenny laughed. "No, Pennington was our landlord's name. Chas had his legally changed after high school. Thought it would get him farther in life than Pacheco." She paused, glancing across the room at her half brother, who was accepting a glass of wine from Jean Luc. "As usual, Chas was right."

"Well, you seem close now," I observed.

She smiled. "We are. After Mom and Dad moved to Scottsdale, Chas and Vivienne were a godsend." She paused. "Dad's health hasn't been great."

"Oh, I'm sorry to hear that." If I recalled correctly, Jenny had come from humble beginnings. Her mother had been a housekeeper at one of the local hotels, and her—and apparently Chas's—father had been a farmworker. I could well imagine years of hard labor in the California sun could take a toll on one's health.

"Thanks. He's doing better in the dry climate." She smiled through the obvious pain in her eyes. "And, of course, the cost of living is a lot lower in Arizona, so that's a plus."

I glanced at Chas, greeting his billionairess wife with air kisses—the scene so far removed from cost-of-living conscious farmworkers that it could have been a different planet.

She must have read my thoughts, as Jenny immediately jumped to Chas's defense. "Oh, Chas helps out whenever he can. In fact, he even got Vivienne to get me a job at Price Digital."

I gave her a reassuring smile. "That sounds very generous of him," I told her.

Jenny relaxed. "Yes, well, that's Chas."

I spied Conchita hailing me from the doorway to the kitchen.

"It was lovely to see you again, but if you'll excuse me, duty calls." I gave Jenny a quick hug and threaded my way through the growing crowd.

Outside, clouds of fragrant steam rose from the paelleras as they were transferred to the six tables, to rest under white cloths. The flamenco guitarist I'd hired began playing a soft, inviting song that lured more guests outside, and I trotted up and down beside the filling tables, handing out bowls of cut lemons and making sure everyone was served a generous portion of the meal.

At the Price-Pennington table, Ava sat between Jenny and Chas, who appeared in godlike sculptural profile, closely examining my best buddy's crescent moon pendant—or perhaps the bosom beneath it. David sat on the other side of Chas, scowling their direction, though whether it was directly in relation to his stepfather or at life in general, I couldn't tell. Alison was commenting on the bottle of Petite Sirah Jean Luc had pulled from our private reserve especially for Vivienne, and Jenny was looking distinctly uncomfortable in her surroundings.

I wondered at her reasons for being in attendance—if it had been Vivienne's idea or Chas's.

I watched as Chas tossed back a glass of the Sirah like it was water, then reached for a refill. The pitcher of ice-cold sangria hadn't been touched. I made a mental note to ready another bottle from the cellar in case Chas flattened the first one before his wife could take a ladylike sip or two.

I worked the tables as the afternoon wore on, making sure my guests were happy. I heard plenty of compliments and was pleased to see that a few of my picnic invitees had taken photos of gorgeous paellas, hopefully to share on their social media pages and tag me as the creator.

As soon as I was sure the guests were satisfied, I snuck a glass of sangria and nibbled on a leg of chicken. The afternoon light was beginning to turn gold as the *flan y fruta* was served.

That was when Bradley Wu waddled up to embrace me. His tweed jacket always has a faint fragrance of Turkish tobacco. Brad was a syndicated food columnist with a large online following. The man had incredible taste buds and a vocabulary to match. He once described the history of wine country as, *What began as a low-budget black and white spaghetti western, evolved into a technicolor widescreen blockbuster with an all-star cast and several self-indulgent musical numbers...*

I could only hope he saw my current offerings as Oscar-worthy dramas and not B-movie musicals.

"Emmy, darling!" he hailed me, throwing air kisses at both my cheeks. "I gorged on your creation, and to compensate, I shall be counting calories all next week. But not all the guests have a full appreciation of your achievement. Would you believe, just a few minutes ago, a very ignorant lady referred to your paella as 'seafood rice.' What a philistine insult to a cultural monument! This paella is the culminating triumph of the baroque imagination, as expressed in the culinary arts." He sighed.

I couldn't help but smile. "I'm so pleased you enjoyed it," I said. "Have a sit down and a sip of my Petite Sirah—it'll tan your tongue into belt leather."

"That, I shall look forward to with great pleasure!" He kissed my hand and went back to his table under the trees.

I spent the rest of the afternoon mingling, chatting with guests, and making sure glasses were never empty. As the sun began to sink below the trees in a watercolor painting of pink, oranges, and delicate purples, guests started to trickle toward the driveway, making their way back to town or, in the case of those who had *really* enjoyed the tasting, calling cars to safely transport them home.

I watched Vivienne and her entourage readying to leave. Vivienne swayed unsteadily on her heels, Alison supporting her with one arm. I noted that Jenny was with them now, taking over the role as designated driver and slipping into the front of the car.

"I hope you enjoyed yourselves," I told Vivienne as I approached.

She nodded, her cheeks slightly flushed. "Quite. The winery is lovely, Emmy," she said, sweeping her arms toward the growing vines.

"Thank you," I told her sincerely. "I hope you keep us in mind for your next event."

She nodded. "Oh, be sure that I will," she said as David held the passenger door open for her. "Hector tells me the Sirah is in limited supply?"

I nodded. "Yes, but Hector's been growing more of that varietal, so we'll be making more limited batches."

She nodded. "Good to know."

It wasn't exactly an order, but I took it as interest.

She got into her seat, slightly less than graciously, and I watched David get into the back seat without so much as a look my direction. If I had to guess, he'd long ago hit his limit of small talk with his mother's crowd.

I waved goodbye to Jenny as I watched the car slide away down the avenue into the gathering dusk.

I found Ava in the kitchen, her heels on the floor beside her as she nibbled bits of leftover flan.

"They gone yet?" she asked.

I nodded. "The lingerers are leaving now. I think Vivienne might have been the last holdout. But," I added hopefully, "she seemed to have enjoyed herself."

Ava held her hand up to slap me a high five. "Nicely done!"

"I couldn't have done it without you," I told her.

"That's true." Ava nodded. "I'm exhausted. How do you think it went?"

I crossed my fingers. "So far so good. I guess we'll really know when booking orders start coming in."

"I saw Bradley scarfing paella like it was going out of style," she said, scooping a bit of caramel up with her index finger. "I hope that means he's planning a good review."

"Ditto." I peeked into the almost empty pan and dipped a finger full of caramel myself. "How did things go at the Price-Pennington table?"

"Now there's a stoic bunch." Ava rolled her eyes. "Lots of pleasantries and small talk. Tennis, bridge, the latest gossip from the club, repeat."

"Any of it about the Sirah?"

Ava nodded. "Chas certainly seemed to like it. I think he was getting a bit tipsy as he told me about his golf handicap," she added.

"The wine wasn't the only thing he seemed to like." I shot her a grin.

"He's a married man, Emmy."

"Who had a healthy appreciation for your cleavage."

"He was admiring my pendant," Ava protested.

"Sure."

Ava gave me a friendly punch in the shoulder. "Please. You know I'm not into the country club set. He's not my type."

I raised an eyebrow her way. "That's not what you said when he pulled up in the sports car."

"Okay, okay. I'll admit, he's hot."

"Even *I* would admit that," I said, ignoring how long it had been since I'd been with a hot guy.

"But he's so pretentious. Every other word was a name drop. I swear the conversation was specifically designed to make me feel intimidated by his enormous…"

My other eyebrow rose.

"…ego," she finished with a sweet smile.

I laughed. "Well, as long as his wife had a good time—"

"And books her next corporate event here," Ava cut in.

"—*and* buys a few cases of Sirah, that's all that matters."

"I'm sure she did, and I hope she will," Ava told me, licking her finger.

I left Ava in the kitchen and made my way to the tasting bar, where I helped Jean Luc with the remains of the party. An hour later, we had the big cleanup done, and the day caterers had been paid, thanked, and tipped for their hard work. Conchita had put away the last of the heavy cast-iron pans, and Hector had doused the outside fires.

I made my rounds, locking doors, turning out lights, and shutting the main buildings down for the evening. I bid Jean Luc good night and closed the tasting room, then made my way to the cave to secure the cellar.

I was just about to throw the big toggle switch that controlled all the lights, when something caught my eye. A broken wineglass sat on the red clay tiles across the room, where rows of oak barrels stood under sandstone arches. I frowned. No one was supposed to be drinking down here. I crossed the room, my heels clacking on the floor as I passed the foot of an old vertical hundred-gallon barrel once used for aging Zinfandel.

Just on the other side, I spied the guilty party. Slumped on the floor sat the drunken blond godling, Chas Pennington. I swallowed down annoyance at the idea Chas thought he could help himself to our private reserves. Especially after guzzling the Petite Sirah as he had.

"Mr. Pennington?" I called. "We need to get you up now."

No response.

"Mr. Pennington?" I said louder. I leaned forward and jostled his shoulder, causing his head to loll backward.

I stifled a gasp as his face turned toward mine. His eyes were wide open, staring at the ceiling in an unseeing gaze, his lips blue, his skin ice cold.

Chas Pennington wasn't dead drunk…he was just dead.

CHAPTER THREE

I was sobbing. I just couldn't seem to stop. Tears and jerky breaths poured from me as I told the short but not-in-the-least-sweet story of how I found Chas again to the young uniformed officer in front of me. He was furiously taking notes on an electronic tablet whose technology seemed to be just a step beyond his abilities.

"And you said he was dead when you arrived?" He hunched bony shoulders as he stabbed at the tablet, doing a pathetic hunt-and-peck.

"Y-yes," I repeated.

"You're sure?"

I nodded, stifling a hiccup.

"Did you check for a pulse?"

I shook my head. "N-no, but his e-e-eyes were open." I pursed my lips together, trying not to recall the image in my head again. Not that I had much choice. I had a feeling the sight of poor Chas's surprised expression would be frozen in my brain for life.

As soon as I'd stopped screaming, I'd run up the cellar stairs to find both Ava and Conchita there, summoned by my blood-curdling cries. I couldn't remember exactly what I said, since I was speaking through my tears and shaking like a second grader on Pixie Stix. But I vaguely remembered telling them both that Chas was dead in the cellar, at which point Ava had called 9-1-1 and Conchita had sat me down in the kitchen with a cup of warm milk. Not that I'd drank any. I couldn't even stomach the thought of water, the image of those wide, lifeless eyes causing bile to rise in my throat.

Thankfully, Ava had been more coherent than I and had been able to give the dispatcher enough information that half an hour later, the winery was filled with uniformed police officers, crime scene techs, and a stout medical examiner who looked as pale as his patients.

"Did you see anyone else in the cellar?" Officer Hunt-and-Peck asked.

I shook my head. "No, everyone had gone home already."

"Everyone except the staff?"

I nodded.

"Had the deceased been drinking?"

I barked out a laugh before I could stop myself. "A lot."

The young officer frowned. "Define 'a lot.'"

I bit my lip. To be honest, I hadn't actually catalogued Chas's consumption. "I-I'm not sure. I was busy. But I know that Ava said he was getting tipsy during the meal."

"That would be Ava Barnet?" he asked, checking his notes.

I nodded again. "Yes. She's a friend. She was here helping me with the event."

Officer Hunt-and-Peck's radio crackled to life at his belt with some indistinguishable code, and he jumped to attention, responding something back that sounded like a lot of numbers and letters jumbled together. Then he nodded my way and walked off to join the rest of the boys in blue wandering around the winery.

I felt tears backing up behind my eyes again. The tasting room had gone from filled with high powered guests to police officers in a matter of hours.

"Emmeline Oak?" a voice asked.

"Emmy," I replied automatically. I wiped my eyes and looked up to find a tall, broad shouldered man standing before me. Unlike the previous police officers, he was dressed in a pair of jeans, black boots, and a button-down shirt rolled casually at the sleeves, instead of the pressed blue uniform. But the air of authority and command were a dead giveaway that he was a member of law enforcement. He looked to be mid-to-late thirties, his dark hair was just a bit overdue for a trim, and his sharp-angled jaw seemed to have a slightly abrasive texture, which betrayed the fact he'd been on the job for several hours now. His eyes were brown, with little golden flecks in the irises that seemed to dance in a frenzy as he quickly took in the scene before him. While the overall effect was easy on the eyes, his strong stance, hard expression, and assessing gaze gave a hint of danger lying just below the tightly contained surface. Something I wasn't keen on tapping into. I shifted on the hard wooden chair as his gaze pinned me.

"Detective Christopher Grant," he announced, quickly flashing a gold badge that confirmed my earlier suspicion of law enforcement. "With the Sonoma County Sheriff's Office. You were the one who found the deceased?"

I took a deep breath, steeling myself to tell the tale again. "Yes."

He pulled a small pad of paper from his back pocket, flipping it open to a page of notes. Apparently he'd not gone digital yet like the young uniformed officer. "You didn't move anything in the cellar?"

I shook my head. "No. I already told the officer there"—I gestured to Hunt-and-Peck—"that I only touched Chas's shoulder. As soon as I saw…" I paused, my throat closing up again. "As soon as I realized he was deceased, I ran."

"And was the wineglass broken when you found it?" he asked.

That question was new. "Yes. Actually, that's what alerted me to the fact that someone had been in the cellar."

He nodded, his eyes flitting to the heavy wooden door. "Any other signs of a struggle that you noticed?"

I blinked at him. "Signs of a… Wait. Chas got drunk and fell, right?"

Grant didn't answer me, instead shooting me a hard, unreadable look. "The deceased was here for some sort of party, correct?"

"Uh, yeah." I licked my lips. "It was a tasting event. But, what did you mean by *struggle*? This was just an accident, right?"

Grant ignored the question. "Who else was at the tasting event?"

"Lots of people."

"Pennington come with anyone?"

I wet my lips again, my mouth suddenly dry. "Yeah. I mean, yes, his wife was here."

"That would be"—he checked his notes—"Vivienne Price-Pennington?"

I nodded, and I inwardly cringed at the name being said out loud. No way was Vivienne going to be a fan of anything Oak Valley related now, no matter how smooth our Sirah was. I silently said goodbye to her future business. "But they arrived separately," I told him. "Vivienne came with her son and mother, and Chas arrived with his sister."

"Jennifer Pacheco." This time Grant didn't have to consult his notes to remember the name.

"Right. Jenny." I paused. "This was an accident, right? I mean, Chas was drunk. We all saw that. He passed out. And…" I trailed off, hoping the detective would fill in that blank for me.

Grant blew a breath out through his nostrils, eyes narrowing at me ever so slightly, as if deciding exactly what information to share. "Mr. Pennington shows signs of having ingested a foreign substance."

"What sort of substance?"

"The ME has not made a determination yet. We'll need to wait for a tox report."

"Tox report…?" His meaning hit me. "Poison? Are you saying Chas Pennington was *poisoned*!?"

The dancing flecks in his eyes hit me with a hard look again. "I'm not saying anything."

Sure. But his silence spoke volumes. I recalled the broken wineglass beside the body. Had Chas's wine been poisoned? I closed my eyes and thought a really dirty word, imagining all those great reviews for my paella now being replaced by headlines about the poisoned wine at Oak Valley Vineyard.

I realized Grant was talking again and opened my eyes, willing myself to tune in instead of lamenting the impending imbalance of Shultz' Seesaw.

"…and we believe Mr. Pennington expired just after 8:00 p.m. Who was at the winery then?"

I tried to think back, but I hadn't exactly been watching the clock at the time. "I-I don't really know. I mean, I think people were starting to leave then. I was outside, saying goodbye to guests. Some people might have been in the tasting room, still, finishing their drinks."

"Was Jennifer Pacheco still here?"

Something in his voice made my head shoot up, my eyes meeting his. They were still unreadable, but I could tell my answer meant something to him. "You don't think Jenny had anything to do with her brother's death, do you?"

"Just answer the question, please, ma'am."

My turn to narrow my eyes. In the South, calling someone "ma'am" might be a sign of respect, but in California the only people who called a woman in her thirties "ma'am" were either being carelessly condescending or purposely rude.

"May I see your badge again, please?" I asked.

If the question surprised him, he didn't show it, instead pulling the badge from his back pocket again and holding it out in front of himself.

I leaned in, taking a good look this time, and felt my heart sink at what it said. *VCI Unit.* Violent Crimes Investigations. This was not an accident. Grant was here investigating a crime…a murder.

"You're a homicide detective."

He didn't confirm or deny the accusation, instead returning the badge to his back pocket.

"What time did the victim's sister leave the tasting event?" he asked.

I noticed Chas Pennington had suddenly gone from deceased to victim. I swallowed a dry lump. I'd kill for a glass of water right about now. I cringed. Ouch. Bad choice of words.

"Ms. Oak?"

"I'm not sure," I admitted. "I didn't check the time. But I know that Jenny had nothing to do with this."

"You know Ms. Pacheco well?" His posture shifted.

"I do." I paused. "Well, I did. I mean, we went to school together. And I know she was devoted to her brother."

"How so?"

"Well, she loved him." It sounded lame even to my own ears. "I mean, she said he helped out with the family. He got her a job with his wife's company. They were close."

"Did you know she was his sole heir?"

That took me aback. In more ways than one. Chas Pennington hadn't been discovered more than an hour ago, and already this guy knew more about him than I did. Clearly Detective Tall, Dark, and Dangerous was not one to be trifled with.

"I-I don't know if Jenny even knew that."

"She did." He didn't elaborate, instead changing gears. "Did you see Jennifer Pacheco leave your event?"

I thought back. "Yes. Actually, she left with her sister-in-law. Vivienne. She drove them." I smiled, pleased to provide Jenny with an alibi. Even though I was sure she didn't need one.

Grant consulted his notes. "Witnesses say Mrs. Price-Pennington left at exactly 8:35."

I wondered who the "witnesses" were. Probably Hector. He was very precise with time. Which, normally, was something I loved about him. In this case, the timing didn't help Jenny much. Especially if her brother was already dead by then.

"We'll be in touch if we need anything else," Grant said, shutting his notepad with finality and shoving it back into his pocket. He extracted a business card and handed it to me. "In the meantime, please call if you think of anything else that might be useful."

I nodded, though I had little intention of calling Detective Grant. The last thing I wanted to do was help him prove that Chas Pennington had been poisoned by a glass of my wine.

CHAPTER FOUR

It was well past midnight by the time the forensics crew left the winery, and I spent a short, fitful night's sleep interrupted by dreams of dead men in my cellar. I awoke shortly after dawn, feeling the tension and physical exhaustion of the previous day in every bone in my body. I thought about working the kinks out with a short morning yoga routine, but I was feeling about as far from Zen as I could be. So I opted for a very hot shower instead, and added extra mascara and eyeliner to try to detract from the bags under my eyes.

I was just pulling on a pair of suede knee-high boots over my jeans and cream-colored silk T-shirt when I got a text from Ava.

At the door. Have coffee.

God, I loved that woman.

My cottage sat toward the back of the main buildings, away from the front drive and nestled among the oak trees. It was small by modern standards, built by my grandfather years before, but my parents had upgraded the plumbing and added AC, so it was comfortable. Plus, with a commercial kitchen just steps away, I never cooked in my own cottage, and it wasn't as if the two bedrooms weren't plenty for me, myself, and I. Even if I did yearn for a larger closet.

I crossed the hardwood floor of the small living room, my boots clacking, and found Ava on the other side of the door, a pair of paper coffee cups in hand.

"You are a goddess," I told her, ushering her inside.

"Tell me something I don't know," she answered with a grin. "Here. I figured you could use this today."

I took a grateful sip. "Have you seen the news today?" I asked.

"That the wine at Oak Valley Vineyard is poisoned? Yeah. I saw it."

I cringed. While I'd anticipated such a headline, I'd been too chicken to actually look. "So much for my put-us-on-the-map event."

"Oh, you're on it," Ava said. "Just for the wrong reasons." She shot me a sympathetic look and put a hand on my shoulder. "Sorry, hon. I know how much it meant to you."

I shook my head, unwilling to let any tears mar my makeup today. "It's okay. I'm sure as soon as the police get to the bottom of this, it will come out that my wine is fine and had nothing to do with Chas's death."

"Do the police have a suspect?"

I thought back to the conversation with Grant. "Unfortunately, I think they might suspect Jenny."

"No way!"

"Way." I told her how Grant had questioned me about when Jenny had left and how she stood to inherit. I'd tried calling Jenny last night, but it had gone straight to voicemail. I had no idea if she still had any family in the area to comfort her, but I could only imagine how hard she'd be taking news of her brother's death.

"How much was Chas worth?" Ava asked.

"Honestly? No idea. I know his wife is loaded, but I have no idea how much of that goes to his sister. If any," I added.

"Maybe we should find out."

I paused, my coffee halfway to my mouth. "What do you mean?"

Ava shrugged. "Just that someone killed Chas, and it would be good to find out who."

"I'm sure the police are handling it," I said, not entirely sure of anything. While Grant was right that I didn't know everything about Jenny, I knew her character well enough to know she wouldn't hurt a fly. If he was looking at her, he was barking up the wrong vine.

"You really haven't seen the headlines, have you?" Ava said, sympathy lacing her voice again.

The coffee suddenly tasted bitter in my mouth. "How bad are they?"

She pulled her phone from the back pocket of her white capris—paired today with a flowing, paisley printed, off-the-shoulder blouse that clung in all the right places. She swiped through a couple of screens, coming up with a piece by Bradley Wu.

Death in Wine Country read the headline.

I groaned out loud.

"Oh, it gets better," Ava warned, scrolling down as I read.

While the paella at the Spanish shindig on the hill was to die for, the main dish was actual death—served up by Oak Valley Vineyard's own Petite Sirah. Thank goodness they only make it in small batches! Forget the long kiss good night. Chas Pennington only enjoyed a sip before dying.

I closed my eyes. I counted to ten. I thought a really dirty word. "Please tell me this is the worst of it?" I squeaked out.

Ava shook her head, her eyebrows drawn down in sympathy again. "I could, but you know I'd never lie to you."

I sighed, feeling those tears threaten my mascara. "What am I going to do?" I asked, flopping back down onto my worn leather sofa. Desperation bubbled up in my throat.

"Well, first of all, you're not going to cry," Ava told me sternly. "The smoky eye thing looks too hot to ruin."

I sniffed and grinned at her. "Thanks. No crying. Check."

"Next," she went on, "we're going to find out exactly how that poison got in Chas Pennington's glass and make sure everyone knows it had nothing to do with your wine."

"And how do we do that?"

Ava smiled, the mischievous grin reaching all the way to her big brown eyes. "What do you say we pay the widow Price-Pennington a visit?"

* * *

While Ava's idea had *harebrained scheme* written all over it, I decided it wasn't entirely a bad idea to visit Vivienne Price-Pennington, if nothing else at least to pay our respects. I had little hope of ever doing business with her now, but maintaining a good rapport was a small step toward repairing my crumbling reputation. And, it wouldn't hurt to at least ask how much money Jenny might stand to inherit now.

We finished our coffee, jumped in my Jeep, and headed west toward the Price-Pennington estate. Fifteen minutes later, I pulled up to the heavy wrought iron gates, standing open, and followed the winding private road up to the big house. I parked under a shade tree in the large drive, and stepped out, my boots' high heels catching on the rough pavers.

"Nice place," Ava said beside me.

"Not bad for a second home," I added as I took in the impressive structure. While it was clearly built with a modern hand, the architecture seemed to be a hodgepodge of previous centuries' styles, with nods to Victorian designs in the roofline, a large Craftsman-style porch, and several sprawling towers and turrets cropping up from the roofline like a miniature castle.

A tall butler in formal-looking attire answered the door, adding to the regal air of the place.

"May I help you?" he asked in a voice that was deep and monotone. The pallor of his skin coupled with the dark circles under his eyes reminded me of Lurch from *The Addams Family*.

"We're here to see Vivienne Price-Pennington," I told him.

He looked me up and down, the only indication that I didn't live up to his standards a slight curl of his upper lip. "Is she expecting you?"

"No," I admitted. "But we'd like to offer our condolences."

He made a noncommittal grunt on the back of his throat but stood aside to allow us entry. "Follow me," he said—a command and not an offer.

We did, Ava and I trailing after him down a series of corridors, our heels echoing in the quiet mansion, until we reached a beautifully furnished lounge where a broad picture window framed a vista of distant mountains, seen across a lush green valley.

"May I offer you a drink while you wait?" the butler asked.

I shook my head, Ava doing the same. "Thanks. We're fine."

"I'll alert Mrs. Price-Pennington to your presence," he said, almost making it sound like a threat more than a promise as he ducked out of the room.

Thankfully, we didn't have to wait long as Vivienne appeared a moment later. It looked as if she'd aged a decade in the few hours since I'd seen her last. If my eyes had bags, hers were carrying steamer trunks, the puffy red skin impervious to makeup. She'd made an attempt at looking presentable, but the coiffed hair and deep red lipstick somehow just served to amplify the grief I could see etched in the noticeable lines on her face today.

"I'm so sorry for your loss," I started, reaching a hand out to her.

She took it, shaking limply. "Thank you. Good of you to come."

"Of course," I told her. "I can't imagine what could have happened to Chas."

Vivienne let out a humorless laugh. "He was drunk, that's what. As usual." She ended the thought with a hitch in her voice, digging into the pocket of her rumpled slacks for a tissue, which she pressed to her nose as she sank into the armchair opposite us.

"I'm so sorry," I said again, sitting on the sofa. I felt Ava shift beside me. "Is there anything I can do?"

Vivienne shook her head. "There's nothing any of us can do for him now. My poor Chas dug his own grave."

Ava shot me a look. "What do you mean?"

Vivienne sniffed again. "Just that he lived hard, looked pretty, and died young." She broke down, a sob escaping her.

"The police were at the winery," I said softly, laying a hand on hers. "They said it looked like Chas was poisoned."

"Lies!" Vivienne's head snapped up. "All lies. Who would ever want to hurt Chas? The man was a living god."

Who lived hard and was poisoned young. Clearly grief was clouding her opinion.

"Did Chas have any arguments with anyone? Any disagreements lately?" I asked.

Vivienne shook her head, shoulders slumping back into her seat. "Just the usual."

"Usual?" Ava asked, jumping on the word.

She sniffed and said, "My family wasn't the biggest fan of my marriage to Chas, and I doubt anyone in this house is shedding tears over him besides me. He was, well, truth be told, a *bit* younger than I am."

"Oh? I hadn't noticed." I'm proud to report I said that with a straight face.

Vivienne gave me a smile. "It was a small point of contention in the family."

"Your son?"

She nodded. "And my mother. They both thought Chas was after my money." She laughed again, the sound coming out on a hacking cough. "I ask you, what were *they* really concerned about? My happiness?" She didn't wait for an answer before continuing with, "No. They were worried about *their* share of the pie. Hypocrites."

"How much of a share did Chas end up getting?" Ava asked.

Vivienne's head shot up. "I'm not an idiot. We had separate bank accounts. Chas had a generous allowance, but that's it."

I thought of the Lamborghini Chas had driven to the vineyard that, incidentally, was still parked in our lot. The allowance must have been pretty generous indeed. A thought that must have showed on my face, as Vivienne continued.

"Look, you didn't know Chas. I gave him gifts from time to time, yes. The car, the gold watch, the Armani suits. But Chas wasn't after my money. He loved me. In fact, it was *his* idea to have a prenup. He didn't marry me for my money. I don't expect you to understand it, but what we had was love. Not business." Then she relapsed into a bout of tearing sobs.

I patted Vivienne's hand awkwardly again and glanced to Ava. This wasn't getting us anywhere, and I had a bad feeling that instead of comforting Vivienne, we were just upsetting her more.

"Did Chas have any close friends? Other family?" Ava asked.

Vivienne shrugged. "He has friends at the golf club. But I don't believe he was particularly close with anyone."

"What about colleagues?" Ava pressed. "Chas worked with you at Price Digital, right?"

Vivienne nodded. "Yes. I got him a managing consultant position after we married."

I was no MBA, but I had a feeling that title was code for *sit in an office and look pretty.*

"How was Chas's relationship with his sister?" Ava asked.

Vivienne looked up, putting her tissue to her nose. "Fine. I don't know. I didn't really know her."

"But you got her a job at your firm too," I pressed.

She sighed and shook her head. "*That* was one thing I should have denied Chas."

"Why is that?" I asked, suddenly fearing this interview might be casting more ill light on Jenny than less.

"That girl is a disaster. No head for numbers. Sadie had to fire her last week."

I felt my heart jump into my throat. Jenny had talked about her job as if it were current. She hadn't mentioned being fired. "How did Jenny take that?"

Vivienne chuckled. "Not well. I caught her begging Chas for money. Again. Of course, Chas was too kind to say no, but I told him he was going to have to cut her off eventually."

I cringed. I could almost see Grant's stoic face making a note of that. Maybe she killed him before he could cut her off. I shoved that thought aside. Someone else maybe. But not the Jenny I knew.

"You mentioned a Sadie?" Ava jumped in.

"Sadie Evans. Yes, she works for me." She paused. "Well, did. I guess she's more of a partner now." The way she said it told me there was some history there, but before I could pursue it, Vivienne continued, "Of course, Sadie never wanted to hire the girl in the first place."

"Why was that?" I asked.

She paused. "I don't know. Sadie wasn't Chas's biggest fan."

It was starting to look like his fan club consisted of one—his wife.

Another thought occurred to me as I remembered the way Chas had been eyeing Ava's "pendant" over lunch. "Is there any chance that Chas may have had…a bit of a wandering eye?"

Vivienne stopped her sniffling and frowned. "Oh no. He didn't hit on you, did he?"

I felt my cheeks color. "Me? No."

Ava wisely stayed silent beside me.

Vivienne shook her head. "Yes, it's true Chas had a healthy appreciation of the female form. What can I say? The man was very virile. One of the things I loved about him. But yes, from time to time, his drive may have gotten ahead of his good sense."

I tried to read between the lines. "You mean Chas was unfaithful to you?"

She waved the comment off. "Not intentionally. But we all make mistakes. I forgave him. He may have gotten caught up in the moment once or twice, but I knew he *loved* me."

"Anyone he may have gotten caught up with recently?" I asked, liking this new angle.

"Of course not," Vivienne snapped.

But the way her eyes suddenly hit the floor afterward told me she wasn't as sure as she sounded. I filed that tidbit of info away for later.

"I saw that Jenny drove you home last night," I said. "Was she with you before that?"

Vivienne shook her head. "No. I don't know where she was. I had a business call I had to take, so I went out to my car for some privacy."

"Alone?" Ava asked.

Vivienne turned to her. "Yes. That's what private means."

Which meant Vivienne couldn't provide an alibi for Jenny.

Though, as I watched her sniffle into her tissue again, I noted it also meant one other thing.

Vivienne Price-Pennington didn't have an alibi for the time of her husband's death.

CHAPTER FIVE

"So, do we buy the grieving widow act?" Ava asked once we were back in the car.

I swatted her arm. "I don't think it was an act."

Ava shrugged. "Okay, so maybe the grief was real." She paused. "But just because she misses the philandering god doesn't mean she wasn't the one who killed him in a fit of passion."

"Poisoning doesn't strike me as something one does in a fit of passion," I mused, as much to myself as to my best friend as I pulled away from the estate.

"Good point." Ava bit her lip, looking out the window as rows of oak trees gave way to the main road. "So maybe one of his little *mistakes* did it. Maybe an affair gone wrong?"

I nodded. "Maybe. But Vivienne said he hadn't strayed recently."

Ava laughed. "Yeah, right. For a corporate type, Vivienne is a terrible liar."

I grinned and shot her a look. "You caught that too, huh?"

"Look, either that woman is lying to herself or us, but I'd bet money Chas had a least one woman on the side. Who knows, maybe more."

"Well if his wife didn't know who—"

"Or isn't telling us."

"—how are we going to find out?"

Ava fell silent, thinking about that for a beat. "You said Chas and Jenny were close, right?"

I nodded. "That was the impression Jenny gave me."

"Maybe she knew?"

I started to shake my head in the negative, as that didn't seem like the type of secret Jenny would keep. But then again, I didn't know Jenny *that* well. Schoolgirl Jenny—yes. But the grown woman who had left out the fact that her brother's wife had just fired her? That Jenny I was still 99% sure had not killed her brother. But how much about his smarmy life she knew, was anyone's guess.

"Maybe we should pay Jenny a visit."

* * *

Fifteen minutes later, Jenny greeted us at the door of her small apartment in a complex near Riverside Drive. Only as she ushered us in, I realized someone else had beaten us there.

Detective Grant stood beside a love seat, his little notebook in hand, his broad shoulders practically filling the room. Or maybe that was just his commanding presence. His sharp eyes honed in on Ava and me, recognition dawning immediately. I had a feeling not much got past those eyes. Today he was dressed in the same style of worn jeans, but he'd paired them with a black blazer with a distinct gun bulge at the hip. It gave him an air of danger that made me shiver despite my innocence.

"Ms. Oak. Ms. Barnet." Grant nodded curtly toward each of us.

"I hope we're not interrupting," I said, my eyes going to Jenny. In sharp contrast to Grant's confident air, Jenny looked much smaller and more pale than the day before. Her eyes were red and looked wet, like tears were her perpetual companion.

"The detective was just asking a few questions," Jenny answered, her voice small and weak in a way that made me instinctively feel protective. She sank down onto an armchair, and I stood behind her, taking a physically protective stance and mentally ready to defend her.

"What sort of questions?" I asked.

Grant's eyes flickered to mine. "About the wineglass that was found near her brother."

Jenny put a hand to her mouth, stifling a sob. "He says Chas was poisoned. Who would do that?" she asked me.

I glanced at Grant. If I had to guess, he thought Jenny would. "What about the glass?" I asked him. "We had several circulating at the event."

"How did Mr. Pennington come by this particular glass?"

I blinked at him. "I don't know. I mean…he probably got it from the tasting room."

"You didn't hand it to him?" Grant asked, his eyes on Jenny now.

She shook her head. "No. Chas had enough to drink at the picnic. I wouldn't have encouraged him to drink more."

Grant consulted his notes. "Yes, several people described Mr. Pennington as intoxicated at the event."

"It was a wine tasting. Several people were intoxicated," Ava pointed out.

"But we made sure they Ubered home," I assured him, again almost feeling guilty under his assessing gaze.

Grant made a sound like a grunt, going back to his notes. "So you didn't handle his glass at any time?" he pressed Jenny.

She shook her head. "I-I don't think so."

"You don't think so, or you're sure you didn't?"

"I don't know," she said, her voice pitching up in a frenzy. "A lot was going on."

"Were you drinking?"

Jenny looked from Ava to me as if searching for the right answer to that question. "I-I mean, a little. I had a glass at the early tasting. Maybe one with the meal. But I had offered to drive Vivienne home, so I only had water the last hour or so."

"Why do you want to know?" I asked Grant.

His gaze turned to meet mine, and I felt myself shiver again. I could well imagine many guilty parties cracking under his hard stare. It was almost as if he could see inside me, could see every dirty little secret I'd ever had, every little white lie I'd ever told. Even if my worst was lying about my weight on my driver license and the fact that I maybe had a little help from Clairol with my particular shade of blonde.

"I want to know," Grant answered, his voice low and even, "because Jenny's fingerprints were on the wineglass."

"I don't know how they got there!" Jenny cried, her protest ending in a sob.

I shook my head. "But the glass was broken. How can you even tell whose fingerprints were on it?"

"We were able to retrieve the larger shards and found two partial prints. The victim's and his sister's." He nodded toward Jenny.

"Well, I-I must have picked up his glass at some point. I mean, we were at the same table. Maybe I grabbed the wrong glass?" Which might have been more convincing if it hadn't come out as a question.

"Anyone could have touched that glass," I said, coming to her defense.

"But only two people did. Just two sets of prints." Grant held up a pair of fingers to illustrate the point.

"Maybe the killer's prints were on the glass that shattered," I reasoned.

"Maybe." Grant didn't sound too convinced.

"Have you looked into Vivienne Price-Pennington?" Ava cut in.

All eyes went to her—Grant's filled with something akin to curiosity, while I was pretty sure mine were flashing with fire. While I knew Jenny was innocent, shoving our biggest VIP under the bus was not the best strategy to win friends in wine country.

"Uh, she, uh, may have had a motive to want her husband gone," Ava said.

"Vivienne?" Jenny choked, her voice laced with tears. "Why on earth would she want that?"

"No reason. Ava is reaching." I shot my friend a look. *Ix-nay on the Ivienne-vay.*

"We are following several leads at the moment," Grant said noncommittally. He shut his notebook and nodded to Jenny. "I'll be in touch."

As he stepped toward the door in the small room, he came within a few inches of me, the heat from his body radiating in a way that felt as if it filled the room. His flecked eyes met mine, and something flashed behind them that made my stomach flip. Danger, distrust, and maybe even a little heat. It was all I could do to keep from confessing my real weight and hair color.

As soon as he left, I felt a collective sigh of relief in the room at large.

"Sorry," Ava said, falling onto the sofa. "I didn't mean to finger Vivienne. That guy just makes me so nervous."

"I understand," I said, meaning it.

"How anyone can be so intimidating and so hot at the same time is beyond me," Ava added.

I shot her a look.

"What? You can't tell me he didn't make your lady bits tingle just a little."

Honestly? I couldn't. So I wisely changed the subject. "You okay?" I asked, turning to Jenny.

She shrugged her bony shoulders. "I don't know how my fingerprints got on the glass," she mumbled. "But I'd never hurt Chas."

"I know," I told her, putting a hand on her back. "I'm sure the detective's questions were just routine."

Ava raised an eyebrow at me. Okay, so maybe I told little white lies on more than just my ID.

"Jenny, can you think of anyone who might have wanted to hurt Chas?" Ava asked.

She shook her head vehemently. "No! Why would anyone want to hurt him? Everyone loved Chas."

I patted her shoulder again, wondering just how many *everyones* we were talking about. "We saw Vivienne earlier," I began, picking my words carefully. "She mentioned that Chas had been unfaithful to her in the past."

Jenny bit her lip. "He didn't mean anything by it," she said, mirroring what Vivienne had told us. "He just…he didn't always think before he acted. You know? And he's always been popular with girls."

"Any girls in particular?" I pressed.

Again she nibbled her lip, her eyes going to the ground. "You promise you won't tell Vivienne I told you?" Her voice was so low it was practically whispering.

I watched Ava scoot forward on the sofa, teetering on the edge of it in anticipation. I had a feeling this was going to be good.

"Pinky promise," I told her.

Jenny sighed. "A couple weeks ago I saw something at work. Between Chas and a woman."

Something clicked in the back of my mind. "Was the woman Sadie Evans?"

Jenny's head shot up. "How did you know?"

"Lucky guess," I lied. "She's Vivienne's business partner, right?"

Jenny nodded. "She is now. But she started as Vivienne's protégé. She's been grooming Sadie for years at Price Digital, and I swear Sadie is like a little Vivienne clone. She has the same shark attitude in the boardroom and even wears the same clothes and does her hair just like Vivienne. It's kind of creepy, really."

"And Chas was cheating on Vivienne with this Sadie clone?" Ava asked.

I thought about the discomfort I'd detected in Vivienne's voice when she'd spoken of Sadie. Having your protégé sleep with your husband would definitely qualify as uncomfortable.

But Jenny shook her head. "No. I mean, I don't really know."

"You said you saw something at work," I prompted her. "What happened?"

"Well, it wasn't anything really. I mean, I don't know if I should even say anything…"

"You should," Ava said, scooting even closer.

"Well, I just saw Chas in Sadie's office, leaning in toward her. Like, close to her. I guess he could have just been telling her something in confidence, but it felt off, you know? Like a little too intimate. I asked Chas about it later, but he blew it off. But then two days later, Sadie fired me out of the blue." She swallowed, sending me a look that pleaded with me to believe her. "She said it was due to 'underperformance,' but I had a feeling she just didn't want me around."

In case she witnessed even more of what was going on between Vivienne's partner and her husband? I remembered

Chas was late to the party because he'd been *held up at work.* I wondered if Sadie was what he'd really been held up with.

"Jenny, why did you make it sound like you still worked at Price Digital at the party?" I asked her softly.

Her eyes misted again. "I'm sorry. I...I was embarrassed. I mean, look at how well you and Ava have done for yourselves. I couldn't even keep the job my brother got for me."

While my heart went out to her, I didn't point out that I hadn't actually done all that much for myself other than try not to run my parents' legacy into the ground. Jenny had enough problems—she didn't need to hear about mine too.

"I hate to have to ask this," I told Jenny, "but Detective Grant mentioned that you were Chas's sole heir."

Jenny's eyes filled again, and she nodded.

"So you knew about that?

She nodded again. "Yes. Chas told me he made a will after he married Vivienne."

"Do you know what you stand to inherit?"

She shrugged. "Honestly? I have no idea. I mean, Vivienne held the reins on the money." She paused. "Chas helped me out now and then when I couldn't make rent, but it was getting harder and harder for him to convince Vivienne to give him cash. I-I can't imagine he had much of his own, you know? I honestly thought he was silly to make a will in the first place. Why should he? He was so young." Her face scrunched up, her eyes filling with tears. "I guess I'm really on my own now," Jenny said, dissolving into sobs.

Ava got up and took Jenny's hand in hers, patting it comfortingly. I went into Jenny's cluttered little kitchen and found what I needed to brew a cup of tea. As I came back with the warm mug, Jenny was sitting on the sofa, with Ava's arm round her shoulders.

"Are your parents coming into town?" I asked, handing Jenny the steaming cup.

"Not for a few days. For the funeral."

I shared a look with Ava, seeing the same sympathy I felt mirrored in her eyes. A week was a long time, and Jenny seemed too fragile to be alone.

"How about you come stay with me for a bit?" Ava said. "In my apartment, above the shop. You can get a lot of crying done, but if you want to talk about anything, well, at least you won't be alone."

Jenny laid her head on Ava's shoulder. "Would it be totally weak of me to say yes?"

"Not at all," Ava promised.

We helped Jenny pack a small overnight bag, and I dropped the pair off at Ava's boutique, where she promised she'd keep an eye on Jenny for the evening.

I was thankful for her big heart—both for the fact that Jenny had someone to cry to and also that if Detective Grant came around again, Ava would be in the protector role.

I just prayed we were protecting the right person.

CHAPTER SIX

After I dropped off Ava and Jenny, I hit the highway for Oak Valley Vineyard. As I passed the rolling hills, lush at this time of year, like a patchwork quilt of pale greens, yellows, and deep emeralds, I thought about Chas Pennington's short but full life. I had to admit, I saw Grant's point in looking at Jenny first. If she'd lost her job, and Chas was running dry as a backup source of funds, she might have been desperate. Especially if Chas's estate really was worth some money. But I had to admit, both Vivienne and her protégé turned business partner had just as much, if not more, motive. While a crime of passion didn't seem Vivienne's style, maybe she'd carefully planned getting rid of her philandering husband. Or, conversely, maybe Sadie was worried about Vivienne finding out about her and Chas and had killed him to keep the affair quiet and maintain her position at Price Digital. Sadie had been absent from the tasting event, but that didn't mean she couldn't have hired someone to do the dirty work for her.

The first thing I saw as I pulled up the tree-lined drive of the winery was a team of men in black jackets that read *CSI* standing next to the shiny yellow Lamborghini Chas had left behind. I pulled up a few feet away and got out as I watched one of them don latex gloves and break the seal of tape over the doors. The others swarmed over it like ants on sandwich crumbs. One guy used an appliance like a small portable vacuum cleaner to suck up every last particle of dust in the car. Others were using little strips of clear sticky plastic film to lift fingerprints off the dash, steering wheel, and gearshift. They took dozens of photos and put every item they found into Ziploc bags.

I stood there for a good few minutes, feeling like somehow someone should be supervising to make sure nothing was damaged. I had a guess the car cost more than most small homes, and the last thing I wanted was for something to happen to it while it was in my care.

"How much longer?" I asked one of the guys.

He shrugged. "Not much. There's not a whole lot to process. This is just a possible secondary scene."

I nodded, pretending I knew what that meant. I assumed it meant Chas was not killed there, which seemed pretty obvious, given the state he was found in.

I shoved that thought down, willing my brain *not* to conjure up the mental image of that particular scene.

"Can I call Mrs. Price-Pennington to pick it up?"

He nodded. "Yeah. We should have it cleared in an hour or so."

I thanked him and headed toward my office in the main building.

First, I left a message with Vivienne's housekeeper that someone could pick up the Lamborghini anytime that afternoon. Then I booted up my laptop and pulled up a search engine, typing in *Price Digital.* A few clicks later, I was looking at a company directory, and I dialed the number for Sadie Evans, listed currently as the company's chief operations officer.

The line rang four times on the other end before a young, pleasant voice answered, "Sadie Evans' office, may I help you?"

"Yes, I was hoping to speak to Ms. Evans. Is she in?"

"May I ask who is calling?"

"Emmy Oak. I, uh, own Oak Valley Vineyards," I told her, trying to come up with a plausible business excuse for asking after the COO.

Though, as it turned out, I didn't need one, as the pleasant voice answered back, "I'm sorry, but Ms. Evans is in Sacramento for the day. Would you like to leave your name and number, and I'll have her get back to you?"

I did, thankful the woman didn't ask what business I had with her boss. I was prepared to spin a story about a wine order her business partner Vivienne had made, but I'd already lied enough that day.

After I hung up, I went back to my laptop, casually checking out what kind of online presence Sadie Evans had. Lots of business articles naming her, mostly as a footnote to something Vivienne had done. A few photos accompanied them, and I had to say, she did look a lot like a younger version of Vivienne. The same auburn hair, though Sadie's was a shade darker than Vivienne's and on the shorter side. She was dressed in similar business attire in the photos, and it might have been my imagination, but she almost looked like she color coordinated her daily wardrobe choices to match Vivienne's. I found a couple of social media pages, but they were mostly boring and underused, consisting of a few vacation photos and congratulations from college friends on her latest promotions. If she had much of a personal life, it wasn't represented online. No mention of kids, a husband, or boyfriend.

Of course, if her boyfriend were married to her boss, I could see why she'd want to keep it on the down-low.

I switched screens and answered a couple of emails, listened to a few messages—mostly from reporters looking for a statement about the murder at the winery—and ignored a small stack of bills. All of which worked up an appetite, as I realized I'd skipped lunch and it was nearing dinnertime already.

I decided on a quick Baked Brie Fettuccini—fast, delicious, and decadent enough to be the type of comfort food my bruised ego needed. I quickly set a pot of water on to boil for the pasta, popped the brie in the oven, and set about the calming work of chopping onion, parsley, and garlic, sautéing it all in a pan on the stove as the mingling scents sent my appetite into overdrive. I was just about to open a bottle of our Chardonnay to go with it, when I heard tires crunch on the drive outside. I stepped out to find the white Rolls gliding into our parking lot. Though, behind the wheel was not Vivienne but her mother, Alison Price. Beside her sat Vivienne's sullen son, David, who stepped from the parked car and immediately put a hand to his eyes to shield them from the setting sun. I wondered if David got out much.

"Mrs. Price," I called, greeting her.

She smiled and walked my way. "Lovely to see you again, Ms. Oak, if even under such unfortunate circumstances."

"I'm so sorry for your loss," I told her.

"Oh, he wasn't *my* loss," she quickly said. "But yes, I'm afraid my daughter is quite broken up over it. David!" she barked, turning her attention to her grandson. "Get that thing washed before it comes home, would you?" She didn't wait for an answer before turning back toward me. "I'm sure those crime scene people have left it an awful mess."

"They seemed very careful," I reassured her.

I watched David scowl behind his grandmother's back and shuffle toward the sports car.

"Hmm." She narrowed her eyes at me, not looking convinced.

"Uh, could I offer you a glass of our Chardonnay before you go?" I asked, gesturing toward the tasting room behind me.

Her expression softened. "Well, I supposed I could take just a moment or two before returning to Vivienne. Lord knows we could all use the drink today."

I smiled brightly at her, leading her by the arm toward the tasting room as I watched David ease himself into the driver's bucket seat and insert the key, roaring the gorgeous little European machine to life. I waved as David reached for the stick shift, causing the gearbox to make crunching and grinding noises. Then, with spurts of gravel from the rear wheels, the car went off down my oak-lined avenue in a blur of chrome and recklessness. After I was quite sure that David had injured none of my beloved oak trees, I joined Alison at the tasting bar.

"I'd apologize for my grandson's rudeness," Alison told me, "but I'm afraid it's all my daughter's doing. She spoiled that boy beyond good sense."

I smiled, making the appropriate clucking noises as I pulled a bottle from the chiller and uncorked it. "No need to apologize. I'm sure he's shaken up about his stepfather as well."

Alison raised one well-plucked eyebrow my way. "Step*father*? Oh my, if Chas wasn't dead already, he'd die hearing you call him *that*."

"They weren't close?" I asked, pouring a glass for Alison, even though I already instinctively knew the answer to that. I didn't think I'd seen David and Chas so much as speak a word to each other.

"No, not in that sense." She took a sip, clearly savoring the citrus and honey notes, rolling them on her tongue.

I found myself inadvertently holding my breath as I waited for her reaction.

Finally she nodded slowly. "Very nice."

I had a feeling that was the most enthusiasm she ever showed.

"You mentioned David wasn't a fan of Chas's?" I said, trying ever so subtly to steer the conversation back to who might have hated Chas enough to want him dead.

Alison shook her head. "Who can blame him, really? Chas was only a couple of years older than David. I don't know what my daughter was thinking when she brought that man home. But I know what *we* were thinking."

"And that is?"

"Gold digger," she said simply, taking another sip. A slightly larger one, I noticed.

"You think Chas married Vivienne for her money?" Even as I said it out loud, I realized what a ridiculous question it was. Everyone but Vivienne could guess that one.

The *well, duh* look Alison gave me said as much. "I'm not one to speak ill of the dead, but that man made a full-time job of spending my daughter's money. It made me sick."

"Did you ever mention this to Vivienne?"

She waved me off. "Repeatedly. But that poor girl was blinded by him."

"He was a good looking man," I admitted. If you went for the Ken doll type.

But Alison shook her head "No, I mean she was blinded by the idea of love. She was so in love with being in love, she couldn't see that rotter for what he was." She shook her head. "She's always been that way. Case in point: her first husband, that Allen lout. Total layabout. Which is where David gets it—it's not from his mother's side of the family, that's for sure."

"Clearly," I agreed, watching Alison put her glass to her lips and let a generous amount of the liquid roll down her throat. I had a feeling I might have to call her a car.

"That man did nothing but knock my daughter up and leech off her good nature. Of course, after she finally had enough and cut him off, he disappeared, never to be seen again. How's that for gratitude?"

"That sounds difficult for David," I noted.

But Alison shook her head. "David has had every advantage a boy can have. He's squandered them all." She took a generous swig again, falling into silence.

"How was Chas's relationship with his sister?" I asked.

Alison shrugged. "How should I know? I barely knew the thing."

And from the tone in her voice, she had no interest in remedying that.

"What about Sadie?" I asked, carefully.

Alison's glass paused on the way to her mouth again. "Sadie Evans?"

I nodded.

"What about her?"

I shrugged. "Just wondering if she had the same opinion of Chas."

"Sadie worked for Vivienne. What she thought of Vivienne's personal life is irrelevant."

"I thought they were partners."

Alison snorted. Very unladylike. I noticed her glass was also empty. "Vivienne *made* Sadie. Anything that woman has is because Vivienne gave it to her." She paused. "Last year Vivienne decided she wanted to spend more time traveling, so she made Sadie a partner and had her take over more of the business. Vivienne has earned that right."

I nodded, feeling as if I'd hit a sore spot.

"But then that ungrateful thing took advantage of my daughter's good nature and tried to worm her way into the CEO's shoes. Essentially trying to push Vivienne out of the company she made!"

Clearly Alison was not a fan of Sadie's. I wondered if it was just due to her riding Vivienne's coattails or if it had something to do with Sadie sleeping with her daughter's husband.

"Do you know how much Chas's estate might be worth?" I asked. "Did he have any money of his own? Any shares of the Price Digital maybe?"

Alison shook her head. "I doubt it. My daughter might have been blinded by love, but she's no fool when it comes to business. I raised her that way." The note of pride in her voice was unmistakable.

I smiled, refilling her glass. "Obviously you did a wonderful job." A little flattery never hurt.

And Alison seemed to agree, relaxing a bit more in her seat. "Well, it wasn't easy. I had Vivienne young, at least by today's standards. I was only just eighteen, and her father left us shortly after that. I raised her on my own. And raised her well," she added vehemently. "I gave her every advantage I never had, and unlike David, *she* made good use of each one—look where it's taken her!"

I had to agree. Vivienne had done well for herself by any standards.

"Anyway," Alison added, downing the contents of her second glass again with gusto. "Viv will cry and moan for a bit, but I'm sure she'll get over Chas. In the long run, this is probably the best thing that could have happened to her."

I decided to be kind and blame her lack of empathy on the Chardonnay.

"Can I get you a ride home?" I asked.

She stood unsteadily on her heels. "Oh. I think maybe that hit my empty stomach harder than I thought."

"I'll call you a car," I promised her, pulling out my cell.

Half an hour later, I'd deposited Alison safely in an Uber with a promise to return the Rolls to the Price-Pennington house the next day, and I was tucked into my cozy cottage with a big bowl of baked brie fettuccini, the rest of the bottle of Chardonnay, and the TV remote as I flipped through the hundred channels of nothing worth watching. I was just about to give up and find a good book to read instead, when I cruised past a familiar face on the screen.

Chas Pennington.

His tanned features filled my television, his bright white smile gleaming as a newscaster's voice narrated the sad tale of his passing.

"*Controversial Californian software billionairess Vivienne Price-Pennington has been widowed by the death of her second husband, former male model Chas Pennington. Sources known to this channel have indicated that Pennington collapsed and died soon after tasting wine at Oak Valley Vineyard, a family-run winery in Sonoma County.*"

I cringed. Whoever said all press was good press had never been on the business end of a murder investigation. I forced myself to listen to the rest of the story.

"*Asked if foul play was suspected, Detective Christopher Grant of the Sonoma County Sheriff's VCI Unit said a full statement would be issued as soon as forensic tests had been completed.*"

The image on the screen changed, and suddenly we were outside the sheriff's office. Grant stood on a set of stone steps, facing a handful of microphones. Even through the million pixels of TV, the hard, determined look in his eyes made my stomach clench, and I sat up a little straighter.

"This is an ongoing investigation, and as soon as the medical examiner has finished his report, we'll issue an official statement."

"Was it the wine that killed Chas Pennington?" one reporter's voice called from the crowd.

"No!" I yelled at the TV. It was as if I was seeing my career flash before my eyes.

But Grant's face remained unreadable. "That is all the sheriff's office has to say at this time."

"No!" I yelled again. "Tell them it wasn't the wine!"

Unfortunately, my TV hadn't magically become a two-way radio, and Grant didn't hear me, instead stepping away from the podium. The shot switched to a couple of newscasters in the studio, who quickly segued into local weather.

I watched without listening, my heart sinking. *Was it the wine that killed Chas Pennington?* That was the takeaway that every wine enthusiast in Sonoma County would be left with. My killer Petite Sirah. I felt tears of desperation pricking behind my eyes.

A soft knock sounded at my door, and I wiped my eyes with my sleeve before getting up to answer.

Conchita stood on the other side, a pint of chocolate-chip cookie dough ice cream in her hands. One look at me must have betrayed my condition, as she said, "I see you saw the news, too."

I nodded, not able to contain the tears any longer, feeling hot liquid streak my cheeks.

"Here. I thought you'd need this." She shoved the ice cream at me, producing two spoons.

I couldn't help but smile through the tears. "Thanks," I told her, meaning it.

She led me back to the sofa, where we both dug in, and she let me vent a string of curse words—most aimed at the situation in general, though I reserved a few choice ones for Grant in particular for not defusing the reporter's question. "He must have known how that looked for me," I told Conchita.

She clucked her tongue sympathetically. "I'm sorry."

I shoved a spoonful of ice cream into my mouth.

"That policeman said they will know more when the tests are done," she said. "I'm sure then they will see it was poison that killed Chas."

"That's only slightly better," I mumbled, on a roll with my pity party. "We're serving poisoned wine!"

Conchita shook her head. "No, someone put it there."

I sniffled, licking chocolate from the corner of my mouth. "Right. Someone other than us." And Jenny, I silently thought.

"I'm sure the detective will find out who," Conchita said, nodding her plump face.

She had more faith than I did. If Grant was so focused on Jenny, someone else was getting away with murder. "You didn't happen to see Chas's sister at the event?" I asked, hoping for an alibi for Jenny. "Right before everyone started leaving?"

Conchita pursed her lips together, scrunching up her nose as she looked at the ceiling in thought. "No, I don't think I did. Not after the meal. I was in the kitchen cleaning up most of the time. Maybe Hector did?" she added hopefully.

I nodded, though I was pretty sure the detectives had already talked to Hector. "Did you see anyone in the kitchen?" I fished.

Again with the scrunchy thinking face. "In the kitchen? No. But I did see a few people milling around outside. That dead man was one of them."

Which wasn't very helpful as far as alibis were concerned. "When was this?"

"Hmmm…maybe about 7:25. 8:00? The sky was just starting to get dusky."

I felt myself perk up. It had to be right before Chas had drunk the poisoned wine. "Did he have a wineglass with him?" I asked.

Conchita nodded. "Sí, he had a wineglass in his hands. A red—I could tell that from far away."

I bit my lip. The Sirah.

"How did he seem?" I asked.

She frowned. "Drunk. He was slurring his words, swaying."

"Slurring his words?" I repeated, jumping on the phrase. "Was he talking to someone?"

"Sí. And he was smoking a cigar," she went on. "The windows were opened, and I could smell it from inside."

"Who was he with?"

"That young man with the shaggy hair. Vivienne's son."

I felt something tingle down my spine. "David?" From all accounts the two were less than chummy. In fact, I didn't recall ever seeing them speak to each other at the event. "Could you hear what they were saying?"

She shook her head. "Sorry. I was too far away. But I saw the younger guy put his arm around the Mr. Pennington's shoulders, like they were friends. Or maybe he was holding him up, supporting him, you know?"

I nodded, liking this more and more. "Then what?"

"Well, I had to wash one of the pans, then I put some of the dishes away…" She trailed off, her eyes blinking rapidly as she recalled the scene.

I resisted the urge to rush her past the mundane details as I waited for her to replay the moment.

"And then?"

"I remembered I looked up, and they were walking away."

"Both of them? Together?" I asked, trying to stem the excitement bubbling up in my belly.

She nodded. "Yes. The younger man still had his arm around Mr. Pennington. They were walking back toward the picnic tables."

To the back of the main buildings. Or, toward the cave, where Chas had been killed just moments later.

David Allen had been the last person to see Chas alive…and maybe even been the cause of his demise.

CHAPTER SEVEN

On Monday morning, I awoke before dawn again, the cool air seeping through the cracks in the drafty windows, swirling the early morning fog around me as I snuggled deeper into my quilt. I tugged it around me as if to ward off all that I feared the day would bring. Finally I gave up the idea of my protective shroud and stumbled toward a searing hot shower. I did the minimal makeup and threw on a pair of jeans, work boots, and a warm navy sweater just as the sun peeked its head above the hills in brilliant swaths of pinks, blues, and delicate violets.

I left my cottage to join Hector in the field, and we started up the hill, walking toward the burgeoning sunrise to inspect the vines. It was a walk I had often taken with my dad as a child. Hector was silent as we passed along the rows, early shafts of light making the dew on the vines sparkle like gems. He paused to pluck the odd berry and rub his thumb along a leaf here and there. He spoke only when we had reached the topmost point of the property, looking down on my lovely acres. Mom and I had sat there the week after Dad passed. She'd been holding back on her own grief to comfort me, a twelve-year-old. My soul was bound up in those glorious ten acres.

"We're going to have a good harvest, Emmy."

"From your lips to His ears, Hector."

He smiled at me. "He's on our side. He's a wine drinker, you know." Hector winked.

I couldn't help but laugh. A good harvest would be a step in the right direction. But the actual harvesting was going to cost us. If fruit came to bear right now, I wasn't sure we had the funding to turn it over. I'd been counting on event bookings to get us through. Which I'd hoped would pour in after the Spanish event, but so far, the phone had been silent. Scratch that—it had been ringing, but only reporters seemed interested in our winery.

As if he could read my thoughts, Hector put an arm around my shoulders. "It will blow over, Emmy. You know how people are. Think of all the drivers who slow down to peek at a car wreck. But tomorrow there will be another wreck, and everyone will forget about us."

Forget about us. That was almost as horrifying a thought as being branded the vineyard that served poisoned Petite Sirah.

"Does your mom know?" Hector asked quietly.

I took a long shuddering breath. "It's hard to know what she knows these days." I gave him a brave smile I certainly didn't feel.

Last year, when my mom had started forgetting little things, I'd just chalked it up to her age, stress, being tired. Then little things had turned into larger ones, like forgetting what day it was or leaving a pie in the oven for hours until it turned into apple charcoal. The day I'd been visiting for Thanksgiving and found her dressed in an evening gown at 3:00 a.m., insisting that Dad was waiting for her at their favorite local restaurant—which had closed down a decade earlier—I knew I couldn't ignore it anymore. My mom was losing her mind. Early onset dementia, the doctor had said.

She'd insisted on going into a home, not wanting to be a burden to anyone, despite the fact I'd assured her over and over again that she was anything but. Family could never be a burden. But, we were both cut from the same stubborn cloth, and despite her protests that I had my own life and career in LA, I'd insisted on coming home. What else could I do? I couldn't let the winery go down on my watch—not after generations of Oaks had kept it afloat.

Now, Mom had her good days and bad days. The good days were almost harder—those moments where she was fully aware of where she was and what was happening to her. Knowing that she was slipping farther and farther away from herself. That someday she'd just slip away completely, and a stranger who only existed in faraway memories would be living in her body.

I shook off the thought, refusing to turn into a tear-stained mess this early in the day. "I called her last night," I told Hector. "Before I went to bed. I told her about the death and that she might hear some news and not to worry. We have it under control."

Hector nodded, tugging that arm around my shoulder tighter into a hug. "We do have it under control. Don't worry. This will all blow over soon."

Soon couldn't come soon enough for me.

* * *

The first thing I did when I got back to the house was call Vivienne Price-Pennington's number. Predictably at this early hour, I got her voicemail. I left a message saying I'd drop the Rolls off at her house later that morning. While I *had* promised Alison the evening before that I'd get the car back to her, I was also hoping to catch David Allen at home. I'd yet to speak to the young man, and my mind had been swirling all night with questions I was dying to ask.

I thought about calling Detective Grant with the information that Conchita had seen David with Chas just before Chas had died, but the more I replayed the conversation in my head, the more I realized what I had was far from a smoking gun. Despite how strained their relationship might have been, they *were* stepfather and son. It was only natural for them to converse. And the fact that they'd been walking in the general direction of the cave was interesting, but it didn't mean David had actually followed Chas down there. Or provided him with his lethal last drink.

I tried to put all thoughts of Chas Pennington's untimely death out of my head as I grabbed a cup of coffee and made my way into my office. I spent the next few hours with my head firmly buried in spreadsheets and paperwork, and by eleven I had a headache brewing from all the negative balances staring at me in glaring red.

I grabbed a quick sandwich for lunch and changed into a cute blue cold-shoulder tunic that brought out my eyes, black skinny jeans, and a pair of nude heels, and then I grabbed the keys Alison Price had left in my care the day before. As I slid behind the wheel of the very expensive Rolls Royce, I was hit with the scent of leather and the faint wisps of Vivienne's perfume. The engine turned over with a gentle purr. Part of me was melting into the luxury of the vehicle, while the other half was terrified to make a move, lest I leave a smudge or scratch that would cost in the five figures to fix.

Twenty minutes of driving well under the speed limit later, I pulled up to the Price-Pennington estate. The same butler in a crisp black and white uniform greeted me at the door and informed me that Mrs. Price-Pennington was still asleep. I glanced at the time. It was almost noon. Someone must have had a worse night than I had.

"Is David available?" I asked the man.

His dark eyebrows rose, as if very few people came calling for David Allen. "He stays out back." He pointed around the side of the estate. "In the guest house."

"Thanks very much," I told him, handing over the keys to the Rolls as I took off in the direction he'd indicated.

While the main house was just this side of decadently enormous, the guest house looked much more similar in size to my own cottage. The same hodgepodge of styles was present here as with the main house though, a Spanish style stucco on the outside of the building, while the wood roof curved in an arch that reminded me of the type of fairy-tale home I'd imagine the three little pigs to come dancing out of at any moment.

I rapped on the wooden door with my knuckles and waited. Movement sounded on the other side, followed shortly by footsteps. Finally the door swung open to reveal David Allen, his hair mussed as if he too had been sleeping in. He was barefooted, dressed in a pair of sweats and a rumpled T-shirt, and he squinted against the noonday sun at me, running a hand through his too-long dark hair to no avail.

"Hi. I'm Emmy Oak. From the winery?" I said. While I'd met him on two occasions now, I realized we'd not spoken a single word to each other, and I hoped he recognized me.

A hope that was quickly realized.

"I know who you are," he stated simply.

"Oh. Good. Well, I just returned the Rolls to your mom, and I thought I'd, uh, stop by and offer my condolences."

"Yeah right," he shot back.

I blinked at him, "Uh, excuse me—"

"Offer your condolences? Cut the crap." His eyes narrowed. "What do you really want?"

I licked my lips. I hadn't expected him to be so direct. Or hostile. He'd seemed surly and bored the times I'd seen him before, but I could tell there was an anger bubbling just below the surface. Without meaning to, I glanced behind me toward the main house, wondering if anyone could hear me from there.

"Well?" David demanded, leaning against the doorframe.

"Okay, let's be real," I agreed. "I wanted to ask you some questions."

"About?"

"Chas."

To my surprise, David smirked. Then he stepped one bare foot back, gesturing for me to come in.

I hesitated, again glancing at the main house and wondering if it was wise to be alone with David here. I suddenly felt a little like the fly asking to hang in the spider's web with him. I took a deep breath, pasted on a smile, and stepped inside.

I wasn't sure what I expected, but the fairy-tale atmosphere ended outside the guest house. The interior was dark, all the curtains pulled. In the center of the room sat a large, plush suede sofa. It took up the bulk of the living room, facing a huge television on the opposite wall. Several gaming systems were attached to it, though the screen was filled with a muted gangster movie at the moment. Guys dressed in seventies garb threatened each other with big guns on a dock late at night. The walls were covered in artwork, mostly dark paintings in various shades of blue, deep indigoes, and violent reds. Discarded clothes littered several surfaces, and a faint scent of marijuana hung in the thick air. While the main estate served as Vivienne's weekend retreat, if I had to guess, David lived here full time.

He sank into the sofa, leaning back in a relaxed pose that seemed designed to make me uncomfortable in its intimacy. At least if the smirk on his lips and dare in his eyes was to be believed.

"So, what do you want to know?" he asked, arms splayed across the back of the sofa.

Never one to be tempted by a dare, I decided to remain standing. "Everyone I've talked to says you and your stepfather didn't get along."

David raised one eyebrow at me in a devilish arch. "Everyone. You mean my mother and grandmother, don't you?"

I hesitated, not exactly sure I wanted to out the two ladies. "So it's true. You didn't get along?"

David shrugged, pushing hair out of his eyes. Up close I noticed he was older than I'd originally thought. The dark, brooding thing he had going on made me think of a teenager, but the stubble on his chin and faint creases at the corners of his eyes told me he was probably closer to my own age.

"Chas and I may have had words now and then," he said, a hint of humor in the statement. "In fact, I thought the guy was a sleaze. Whoever killed him did us all a favor."

Ouch. "All of you?" I said, jumping on his wording.

David shrugged again. "I can't imagine my grandmother made a play at grief with you?"

I shook my head. "No, she was pretty…"

"Blunt?" David provided. "Yeah, that's her. You never have to guess what's on her mind." He looked up at me and gave me a self-deprecating smile. "Lucky me, right?"

"Who else did Chas's death favor?" I asked.

"Take a number. I hear his sister was his sole heir."

"You hear?" I wondered if Detective Grant had been here to question David Allen already too.

David grinned. "I can have secret sources too, Emmy."

My name on his tongue simultaneously felt sensuous and dirty at the same time. It wasn't just his too-intimate relaxed posture. Everything about his manner seemed designed to make me feel uncomfortable. I wondered if it was deliberate toward me or the way he dealt with life in general. I inadvertently took a step toward the door.

"Your mother seemed broken up," I stated, watching his reaction.

David's eyes met mine, and for a moment I could see genuine compassion there. "Yeah. Viv really loved him."

"Viv?"

He gave me wry smile. "'Mom' was never in my vocabulary. In the corporate world, kids are death to your career. Especially in tech in the nineties. Heaven forbid people would think Viv was maternal." David reached into a little wooden box on an end table by his sofa and pulled out a hand-rolled cigarette. "You don't mind, do you?" he asked, putting it to his lips.

I shook my head, though I had a feeling he would have lit it either way.

"It helps with my anxiety," he mumbled, the cigarette bobbing up and down. "Difficult childhood, you know." He grinned, as if sharing a joke, then lit up while I formulated my next question.

"Is there any reason in particular *you* didn't like Chas?"

David took a big puff, and I could tell from the smell it wasn't a tobacco cigarette. Musky, funky air came out as he exhaled. "I can think of a few. He ran through my mom's money like water." He paused. "Excuse me—he was running through *my* inheritance. I forgot we were being real here."

"Didn't your mom have him on an allowance?" I said, thinking back to my conversation with her.

David laughed out loud, his dark eyes dancing at me. "Who sold you that load of bull? Chas?" He shook his head. "Sure, he had an allowance, but all the boy wonder had to do was ask, and cash appeared. He was good like that." He winked at me.

I ignored it, wondering why Vivienne had led me to believe Chas had little access to her money. Had she been embarrassed by the fact she'd given Chas anything he asked for? Or had she been trying to hide something more?

"What do you mean, Chas was good like that?" I asked. "You think Chas was playing Vivienne?"

"Oh, I don't think it. I know it." He took another puff, offering the cigarette my way.

I shook my head, waiting for him to exhale before continuing.

"Chas knew exactly the right buttons to push," he said. "The right moments to play the doting husband, the sympathetic ear, the generous lover."

The way his eyes dug into mine at that last line made my insides squirm. I suddenly yearned for the fresh air and the safety outside the door.

"Chas also knew," he continued, "the right moments to play hurt, offended, and pout until he got his way. Viv was eating out of the palm of that gigolo's hand."

"Gigolo? So you think Chas was cheating on your mom?"

David shot me a look, the wry grin back. "What do you think, babe?"

"I think you call me 'babe' again, and you'll be singing soprano."

David threw his head back and laughed. "Point taken. *Ma'am*." He did a mock salute, but the way he ended it in a grin that made me think he was picturing me naked took all the vim and vigor out of it.

"What were you and Chas talking about at the Spanish event?" I asked, getting back to my reason for being there.

His eyes met mine, some of the humor leaving them. "It was a long event. We talked a lot."

"Odd, considering you couldn't stand him."

"I never said that," David corrected. "I said he was a sleaze who knew how to play Viv like a fiddle. I had to admire that to an extent."

"You were with him right before he died."

One of his dark eyebrows rose up into his long bangs. "Is that what this is about? The cast-aside son kills the young stepfather in a fit of jealousy?"

My turn to raise an eyebrow. "Is that how it went down?"

He rose from the sofa, and I realized just how tall he was. I'd mistaken his lean frame for skinny from a distance, but up close I could tell it was all sinewy muscle. He took a step toward me, the humor disappearing from his face, replaced with an intensity that had me taking another step backward.

"No," he said, softly. "I didn't kill Chas."

Which was exactly what he would say if he *had* killed him. "You were chatting with him outside the kitchen after the meal. About what?"

He shrugged. "Life. Love. Blondes." He gave me a meaningful look that was hard to ignore in close quarters.

"Chas had been staring at your friend's…*assets*…all afternoon," David went on. "I was just reminding him that my mother has eyes. If he wanted to stay in Lamborghinis and Rolexes, it would behoove him to do his staring in private."

"Why would you want to help him stay in your mother's good graces?"

Again with the shrug. It seemed to be his go-to gesture. Or maybe apathy was just his overriding emotion in life. "Like I said, he knew how to play Viv. I happened to need something from dear old Mom, and I had a feeling he could help me get it."

"What did you need?"

He shot me that same wry grin. Okay, maybe David had two go-to looks. "What does anyone need from Viv? Money."

I suddenly felt sorry for Vivienne. You know, unless she was a murderer.

"So you see, kid, I didn't have a motive to want my *stepfather* dead." David infused the words with sarcasm as he flopped himself back on the sofa again.

My body let out a sigh of relief at the sudden physical distance. "No motive, except that he was running through your inheritance."

The smirk returned to David's face. "Yeah. There's that."

"Where did you go after your chat with Chas?" I asked, fishing for an alibi.

He fiddled with the cigarette again, his eyes not meeting mine. "Here and there. Had a drink. Went outside for a smoke."

"And Chas?"

"He said he was going to track down more of that private reserve of yours. He headed toward the cellar."

"Alone?"

David nodded. "And alive."

Though not for long.

I wondered if I believed him. David seemed as if every move was designed to get a reaction out of someone. The rebellious long hair and dark clothes to get a rise from his mother. The overly familiar manner he had with me to throw me off my game. I wondered what front he'd played with Chas. Overly chummy? Pretending to look out for Chas's interests, all the while stabbing him in the back? Or, in this case, poisoning his drink?

As far as I could tell, David Allen didn't seem to have a job. And he lived on his mother's estate. However casually David Allen spoke about Chas now, if the dead man really had been running through Vivienne's accounts, he posed a serious threat to David's standard of living.

"Was there anything else?" David asked, leaning his arms across the back of the sofa again. "Or do you just enjoy my company too much to leave?"

I cleared my throat. "Uh, no. Thanks." I turned and awkwardly fumbled with the door.

"Come by any time, Emmy," I heard David call before I escaped into the fresh air.

I took a big gulp, wondering if the contact high was to blame for the squirmy feeling in my stomach that followed my name on David's breathy voice again.

Conflicted squirms and marijuana mist aside, one thing was for sure—David Allen had ample motive and opportunity to want Chas dead.

And one very shaky alibi.

CHAPTER EIGHT

As soon as I left the not-so-storybook dwelling of David Allen, I called Ava and begged a ride from her. Friend that she was, she said she'd be there in ten.

I'd just hung up with her, walking down the graveled drive toward the main road, when my cell rang again. It was an unfamiliar number with a 408 area code. Considering every well-funded wine lover in Silicon Valley lived within its boundaries, I picked up.

"Emmy Oak," I answered.

"I'm returning a call," came the female voice on the other end. "Sadie Evans."

The mentee-slash-mistress. "Yes, thanks for getting back to me, Ms. Evans," I told her, juggling the phone to the other ear as I glanced back at the house, as if expecting Vivienne, David, and the butler to be eavesdropping. "I was hoping to discuss some…business with you," I said.

"What sort of business?" Sadie asked, not letting me get away with skirting the issue.

"I, uh, own Oak Valley Vineyard," I started.

"The winery where Chas was killed?" she quickly interrupted

I cringed. Were we to forever be known as that? "Uh, yes," I admitted. "I was hoping to clear up one or two little points with you. About Chas." I held my breath. Clearly she had no obligation to talk to me. But I hoped by being vague enough, it spurred her guilty side to curiosity about what, exactly, I knew. Assuming she felt guilt about sleeping with her partner's husband. "I was hoping we could speak in person?" I pressed.

The only sound I heard on the other end was the white noise of a bad cell connection. Then finally, "I'm driving from Sacramento right now. I'll call you when I get into Sonoma."

I was about to ask when that would be, but she ended the call before I had the chance. Not quite a hard meeting date, but beggars couldn't be choosers.

Nine minutes later, true to her word, Ava pulled up along the main road in her prized 1970s olive green convertible Pontiac GTO. She leaned one tanned arm out the window, her hair pulled back in a ponytail that kept it from flying into her eyes, covered in a pair of shiny aviator glasses, looking like a movie star from a bygone decade. "Need a lift, stranger?"

I grinned. "Thanks." I climbed in and glanced in the tiny back seat. "No Jenny?"

"She offered to watch the shop for me," Ava said, hitching a U-turn.

"How's she doing?" I asked.

"Better," Ava promised. "Still going on crying jags now and then, but it's not the full-on waterworks of yesterday."

"Sounds like it was a rough night?"

Ava nodded. "A two-pinter of double chocolate fudge. I even had to bring out Meg Ryan. With both Tom Hanks *and* Kevin Cline," she said, referencing two of our fave feel-good movies. "But, like I said, she's doing better today."

"Glad to hear it," I said, meaning it.

"So, what were you doing at the Price-Pennington estate?" she asked, giving me a sly side-eye. "Digging up more dirt on the deceased?"

"Sort of," I admitted. I filled her in on Conchita's eyewitness account on Chas's last moments and my chat with David Allen.

"That guy's a little dark, right?" Ava said.

"You know him?"

"Not well," she admitted. "But I've seen his work at a gallery showing before in town."

"He's an artist?" I asked, thinking of the paintings I'd seen hanging in the guest house.

She nodded. "Not half bad either. Gritty stuff. Not really to my taste, but it's good. Kind of creepy. But I guess that's the point of that kind of art. To get a rise out of people. Make them feel uncomfortable."

I could well see that being David's thing. "David said he saw Chas going down to the cave alone," I told her.

"So, if he's telling the truth—"

"That's a big if," I added.

"—big *if* he's telling the truth, someone must have seen Chas and followed him down there."

I shivered at the thought. Bad enough someone had killed Chas, but the idea of them stalking him like prey was downright scary. Especially since the stalker had to have been one of my guests.

We rode in silence the rest of the short drive to the winery, but as soon as we pulled up the long oak-lined drive, Ava let out an "Uh-oh."

I followed her line of sight to see a large black SUV parked near the entrance. Instead of pulling into a well-marked parking space, the driver had left it just outside the door to the main building, sideways across three spaces. The entitlement and air of authority could only bring to mind one person.

"Isn't that Detective Grant's car?" Ava said, voicing my thoughts.

I nodded. I couldn't imagine why he was here, but when a violent crimes detective was at your door, it was never good.

We walked into the tasting room to find Grant standing at the bar and Jean Luc behind it, his usually reserved countenance thrown into a mess of waving hands and wild gesticulating in the unnerving presence of Detective Grant. At least I wasn't the only one he set off balance.

"Emmy, zank goodness you are here!" Jean Luc said, his French accent more heavily pronounced than normal. "Zis policeman says he needs our wine!"

I turned to Grant. "Our wine?"

"Ms. Oak. Ms. Barnett. Nice to see you again."

"Wish I could say the same," I told him, feeling a frown between my eyebrows. It was one thing to have crime scene techs crawling all over my cellar. But messing with my wine? This was getting personal. "What's going on here?"

Grant produced a folded piece of paper from his jacket, handing it to me. "This is a warrant to search the premises. It includes inspecting all of the wine that was served at the event where Chas Pennington expired."

"Expired?" I took the papers from him. "Geez, he wasn't a carton of eggs," I mumbled.

I thought I detected a hint of a smile from Grant, but it might have been my imagination.

I quickly glanced over the papers, seeing lots of legal mumbo-jumbo that would likely have Seesaw Shultz peeing his pants. "What exactly are you looking for?"

Grant's eyes went from me to Ava, as if not sure how much to divulge. Finally he relented. "Chas Pennington died from ingesting poisoned wine."

There it was in plain English. The headlines were right. Oak Valley Vineyard's wine had killed him.

"Poisoned with what?" Ava asked, stepping forward. "Clearly it wasn't the *wine* itself that killed him."

Grant nodded. "Correct. Preliminary toxicology results came back that a large amount of alprazolam was in the victim's system."

"Alpra-what?" she repeated.

"Alprazolam. It's an antianxiety medication, often sold under the brand name of Xanax."

Ava rolled her eyes. "Why didn't you just say Xanax then?"

Grant pinned her with a look that paused her eyes mid-roll. I felt immediate sympathy for her. I'd been on the other end of that look before. It was not comfortable. Enough to make one need a Xanax, even.

"So you're saying Chas mixed his Xanax with wine and died?" I asked, jumping in to save her.

"Not *his* Xanax. As far as we can tell, he was never prescribed the drug."

"And a legit prescription is the only way to obtain Xanax," I countered, heavy on the sarcasm.

There was that hint of a smile again. If I didn't know better, I'd say I was amusing the detective. Too bad I couldn't say the same thing. The only thing I felt in Grant's presence at the moment was annoyance. And maybe a little danger in the way his broad frame loomed over me. And possibly a little heat from the way the flecks in his eyes danced when he hinted at humor. I wondered what it might feel like to be the recipient of a full-on smile from him. I could imagine the *little* heat erupting into a full-blown lava flow rushing over my body.

I shook the image from my mind, as I realized Grant was talking again.

"...is dangerous enough on its own, but it's even more so when mixed with alcohol," he said. "When drug molecule meets ethanol molecule, the two amplify each other's effects. Working together, they can cause a person to become tired or confused, fall over or pass out. With high enough levels of each, the combined effects would slow down the system enough that it starts shutting off. With enough in the system, one would go into a coma and die."

My skin felt cold imaging Chas's final moments, feeling his body grow from sluggish to unmanageable to the point where even his breathing was too much for him. "So this was an accidental overdose after all?" I asked, ever hopeful.

Grant turned his attention squarely toward me. "Plasma concentrations in patients who are under average treatments for anxiety symptoms show less than a hundred micrograms per liter. Personally, I've seen a level of up to three hundred in addicts. Anything over three hundred is concern for an overdose."

"How high was Chas's?" I asked, hoping to cut the macabre science lesson short.

"Five hundred micrograms per liter."

"Holy moly," Ava mumbled behind me.

Grant's mouth twitched, as if wanting to smile again. Luckily, he was such a stoic guy he was able to keep it in check. "His blood alcohol was also pretty impressive."

"So this was *not* an accidental overdose?"

Grant shook his head. "No. Someone deliberately gave Mr. Pennington a lethal dose."

"Zis iz a nightmare. Zis iz terrible." Jean Luc was flapping his hands again and muttering half in French and half in English.

I tried to ignore him, focusing on the important parts of what Grant was saying. "How long would it take this Xanax and alcohol combination to kill Chas?"

Grant cocked his head in my direction, as if surprised by the question. "You mean, when did he ingest the lethal dose?"

I nodded.

"The ME's estimate is about an hour and a half to two hours between ingestion and death."

I froze, realizing we'd been going about things all wrong. I'd been looking for who could have followed Chas down to the cave. Truth was, his killer could have been anywhere by then. Chas had likely been poisoned long before. In fact, anyone could have slipped the lethal dose into his wine earlier. At the tasting. At the meal. During drinks afterward.

I swallowed a dry lump in my throat. "So why are you taking our wine?" I asked, gesturing to the search warrant in my hands.

Grant shook his head. "We need to check the premises for any residue. We'd like to examine any bottles that were out then. And anything that might have been opened. It if wasn't out that day, we don't need to see it. Just what the public might have had access to."

I breathed a sigh of relief, glad Jean Luc was overreacting on that point.

"But we'll need to look through the kitchen, the glassware, any open bottles or trash on the premises."

I nodded. As far as I was concerned, he could knock himself out with the trash.

* * *

I told Jean Luc to take the afternoon off, before he flapped himself into a tizzy, and asked Hector to keep an eye on Grant and the two uniformed officers who showed up after him, presumably to execute the dirtier aspects of the warrant. Ava offered to stay for moral support, but I figured Jenny and the shop needed her more. I thanked her for the ride and promised to make her dinner soon as a real thank-you.

I left the boys in blue crawling all over my tasting room and ducked into my private office to try to get some work done. A task that was harder than it seemed. Instead of paying attention to the red numbers all over my spreadsheets, my mind kept drifting to Chas Pennington, his time of death, and that fact that no one could have had an alibi for it. Any one of my VIP guests could have killed the playboy. Though a few in particular seemed more likely than the others.

David Allen could easily have slipped the drugs into his stepfather's drink at any point in the evening. I thought back to the marijuana cigarette he'd been smoking for his anxiety. Did he also have a Xanax prescription for the condition? He'd been sitting right next to Chas at the luncheon, with easy access to his stepfather's drink. And Chas had been paying far more attention to Ava's cleavage than to David. In fact, I didn't think anyone had paid much attention to David.

Vivienne, on the other hand, had had Ava's full attention, but even she might have been able to slip away to quickly add a little something extra to her husband's drink. And Chas wouldn't have thought twice about his wife handing him a glass of wine.

Though, at some point in the evening, I don't think he would have thought twice about anyone handing him anything in the wine family. He'd been more than helpful to his killer, guzzling whatever was put in front of him. Had they known him well enough to know he'd do just that?

And then there was Sadie Evans. While she hadn't personally been at the event, it didn't mean she hadn't used her influence and ample funds to convince someone else to do the dirty work for her. Let's face it—every person at the party could have been the killer.

I gave up on the spreadsheets, finding the combination of a dead body *and* a dying bottom line too depressing. On a whim, I opened a search engine and typed in Chas Pennington's name. In contrast to my search for Sadie Evans, I found plenty to wade through. Several social media pages, all very active and mostly filled with selfies. Chas smiling into the camera behind a pair of sunglasses at the beach, posing with a pine tree backdrop in snowy Tahoe, laughing on a yacht somewhere tropical looking. Any one of them could have been in a magazine. I could see how he'd been a successful model prior to meeting Vivienne.

I scrolled through a few pages, not learning much more about the playboy other than he went on an extraordinary number of vacations, liked the finer things in life, and had precious few photos of his wife on his pages.

Without thinking about it, I typed another name into the search engine: Christopher Grant. His official bio on the Sonoma County Sheriff's Office page came up first. Raised in the Bay Area, graduated from Berkeley, recently transferred from the San Francisco Police Department's homicide division. I wondered why. Seemed a step down to be going from homicide detective in the city to violent crime in the usually sleepy wine country. Was this a demotion?

Social media was scarce for the detective, though I did find a couple of articles in online news outlets briefly mentioning him. Always in glowing terms, talking about the criminals he'd taken off the street.

"Ms. Oak?"

I jumped about a mile at the deep male voice calling my name from the doorway. I looked up to find Grant's frame filling it, and I immediately shut my laptop as if I had been caught with my hand in the cookie jar. Or fingers tapping into his personal business.

"Yes?" I asked, hoping my voice didn't sound as guilty as I felt.

"We're wrapping up upstairs."

I nodded. "Good. Great." I paused. "Find anything?"

"I'm not at liberty to discuss that." The man had an excellent poker face.

I blew out a breath. "I don't suppose you're at liberty to discuss what you're hoping to find either?"

His expression softened, and he shook his head.

"Jenny didn't do this," I told him.

He leaned against the doorframe in a deceptively casual pose. "How well do you know her?"

"We went to high school together."

"That seems like a long time ago."

"Was that an insult?"

His poker face cracked, showing a hint of a smile. "Not at all. I'm just saying people can change quite a bit in a...*couple* of years."

My turn to smile. The attempt to cover his inadvertent gaffe could have been kind of charming. You know, if he wasn't wearing a gun. "Jenny had no reason to want her brother dead," I reasoned.

"And you think someone else did?"

I nodded. "I do."

"Okay, who?"

I paused, not sure how much to share. But at this point, it could only help Jenny. "David Allen, for one."

"The victim's stepson?"

I nodded. "He thought Chas was a gold digger, and he was one of the last people to have seen Chas alive."

Grant nodded. "Go on."

I couldn't tell if he was taking me seriously or just indulging me, but I forged ahead.

"There's also his wife. Did you know he cheated on her?"

Grant raised an eyebrow. "I thought Vivienne was a client of yours."

"She is. Or, I had hoped she would be." I noticed he hadn't answered my question.

"But you're throwing her to the wolves to protect someone you knew in high school?"

I crossed my arms over my chest. "I'm assuming the *wolves*," I said, giving him a pointed look, "will only attack if she's guilty."

"And if she's innocent, she'll come sip Merlot from you again?"

I scoffed. "We don't serve Merlot."

That smile hinted again. It was a good look on him. It softened the danger aspect just enough that something more human glinted underneath it.

"Why did you move to Sonoma?" I blurted out.

"Excuse me?" Grant's eyes snapped up to meet mine, all smiles gone, something a lot like anger flashing behind them.

I cleared my throat. "I, uh, heard you're new to the Violent Crimes Unit." I felt my laptop practically thumping like a telltale heart on the table.

"You heard." It was almost an accusation. "You mean you investigated me."

I squared my shoulders, willing myself not to crumble under his tough guy act. Okay, chances were it was not an *act*. He struck me as an actual tough guy.

Luckily, I was something of a tough gal myself.

"Yes. I did. Tell me you haven't investigated me?"

He stared at me, his expression unreadable. "Emmeline Oak. Prefers to go by Emmy. Average student, voted most likely to marry young. Which makes your classmates all wrong, because you're single, no kids, no attachments."

I shifted in my seat, somehow feeling much too vulnerable under his scrutiny as he went on.

"Attended culinary school at the Culinary Institute of America in Napa Valley."

"Which, by the way makes me a member of the CIA," I joked, trying at levity to cover my increasing discomfort that he knew so much about me.

But a small smile was all I got as he continued. "Graduated top of your class, though you've never had a job cooking in a restaurant, as far as I could find. Some private chef gigs, mentions of a few pop-up restaurants in Los Angeles. My guess is you prefer working for yourself. Control freak."

I let out an unladylike snort. "Look who's talking."

"Touché." The corner of his mouth curved up into a full, genuine smile. The movement totally transformed his face, his eyes going from dark to mischievous, creasing with humor and character.

"My turn," I said, feeling a bit emboldened by the softer look. "You're single—no ring," I explained.

He glanced down at his unadorned left hand and gave me one raised eyebrow of admiration at my amazing powers of observation.

"You're something of a workaholic—I can tell by the fact you're never properly shaved."

His hand went to the stubble on his chin.

"And, I'm guessing you burned out in San Francisco and decided to move to wine country for a slower pace of life. Escape the rat race of the Bay Area."

"Sure. Let's go with that."

I tilted my head to one side and studied the flecks in his irises. There was definitely more to that story, but I had a feeling I wasn't getting the unedited version today.

He opened his mouth to say more, however, my cell chose that moment to chirp from my purse.

I gave him the universal one-finger *wait* sign and checked the readout. Sadie Evans.

"Uh, I'm so sorry. I have to get this…" I trailed off, hoping he took the hint.

"Important business?"

If he only knew. "Yeah."

He nodded. "We'll show ourselves out."

Which seemed only fair since he'd shown himself in. With a search warrant no less.

I waited until he was down the hall before answering my phone. "Hello?" I said, catching it just before it went to voicemail.

"Sadie Evans," she announced. "I'm back in town. I can meet you in thirty minutes."

"Do you know the Half Calf?" I asked, referencing the coffee shop next door to Ava's boutique.

"On Main?"

I nodded into the phone. "That's the one."

"I'll be there. Half an hour," she repeated. Then she hung up.

I grabbed my purse and headed for the door, hoping like anything that I didn't run into Grant and his dumpster divers. Because I wasn't in the mood to explain where I was off to.

CHAPTER NINE

The Half Calf was a small coffee shop struggling to maintain a foothold against the larger national chains. Their logo featured a cartoon cow enjoying a latte while lounging on a crescent moon, and their specialty was a caramel-hazelnut latte, which I ordered as I scanned the small groupings of tables for Sadie Evans. I spotted her almost immediately, sitting at a corner table near the back of the shop, her eyes glued to her phone as her finger tapped away on the small screen. She was as slinky as a cheetah, in a dove-gray tailored suit, tastefully done French nails, and the kind of sleek, highlighted hair that spoke of hours in a hairdresser's care.

I grabbed my coffee from the barista and approached her table. I noticed she hadn't bothered with a drink herself.

"Sadie Evans?" I asked.

She looked up, giving me an undisguised once-over. "You're Emmy Oak?"

I nodded.

"Sit." It was a command and not an offer. I had a feeling she made for a very demanding COO.

I sat, sipping my hot beverage as a stall to my opening pitch. Which, as it turned out, I didn't need, as Sadie got right to the point.

"What did you want to talk to me about?" She set her phone down, giving me her full attention. I could see *time is money* being etched into stone as this one's epitaph.

Okay, I could be direct too.

"Chas Pennington," I replied.

"So you said on the phone. What about him?"

"For starters, he's dead." I watched her reaction carefully.

But if I'd expected any grief from her, I was sorely disappointed. She barely blinked a false eyelash at me.

"So I heard." She was beyond cool—she was mentholated. Reminded me of an actress friend I'd had in LA, Hannah Pratt, who'd claimed sex was highly overrated because it always ruined a great hairstyle.

"The police are investigating it as a suspicious death," I went on.

She arched one well-filled eyebrow at me. "And what, pray tell, does that have to do with me?"

"For starters, it may well come out that you were sleeping with him," I said. Okay, I was taking a bit of a stab without evidence, but I trusted Jenny's gut on this one.

A move that proved to be fruitful as she answered, "Were. Past tense."

Bingo.

"So, you *were* having an affair with Chas?"

She blinked at me. "I just said that, didn't I?"

"Did Vivienne know?"

Sadie let out a sharp bark of a laugh. "God, no. That woman was as blind as a bat with cataracts where Chas was concerned."

"Even though you all worked together?" I asked. I found it hard to believe Vivienne hadn't caught on. While I knew love could blind a person, Vivienne had been a self-made millionaire by the time she was thirty. The woman was no dummy.

"Look, if Vivienne knew, she never said a word to me about it," Sadie responded.

"You mentioned the affair was past tense. Chas ended things?"

"*I* ended things," she clarified, her eyes narrowing.

"May I ask why?"

Sadie smirked. "I have a feeling you're going to anyway." She paused, let out a sigh, and craned her neck to the side with an audible crack. "The sex was fantastic, but after a while the complications just weren't worth it."

I knew she was a Hannah Pratt. "What kind of complications?"

"Look, Vivienne is getting older. She can't keep up with the new tech anymore. Her ideas are old school, and so is her coding. It's time for her to retire."

"I haven't heard Vivienne mention anything about retiring."

"You wouldn't. Because she won't do it. She's stubborn like that."

If someone was trying to force me out of my own company, I might be stubborn too. But I kept that thought to myself, instead asking, "How so?"

Sadie shrugged. "She wanted things her way or the highway. But the truth is, she doesn't run anything there anymore. Everyone reports to me, she comes in for board meetings and confuses every issue, and then she leaves me to clean up the mess again."

Which sounded like an interesting dynamic and possibly a good amount of animosity between the two partners, but it didn't explain why anyone would want the boy wonder dead. "Where did Chas come in?"

"Chas was Vivienne's little lap dog. He may have been sleeping with me, but his heart was in *Vivienne's* purse." She shrugged again. "I got tired of him taking her side."

I took a sip of my latte, wondering just how tired of it she'd been. Tired enough to kill him over it?

"And before you think I had anything to do with Chas's death," she went on, practically reading my mind, "there are plenty of people with a much better motive than petty jealousy."

Now we were getting somewhere. "Such as?" I asked, taking her bait.

A gleam hit her eyes that could only be described as wicked. "Poor Vivienne really didn't know what her boy was up to, did she?"

"And what would that be?" I pressed.

She shook her head. "Chas Pennington was like an Easter egg, all wrapped in gold foil. But once you'd scratched off some of the foil, you could smell what was underneath. And that egg was rotten."

As much as I enjoyed a good metaphor, I couldn't stand her drawing it out much longer. "What was Chas Pennington up to that could have gotten him killed?"

"Cards," she said.

"Cards?" I asked. "Like, gambling?"

Sadie nodded, the wicked gleam practically radiating off her as her red lips curved into a smile. "Poker, to be precise. I guess the life of the rich and idle was too boring for Chas. He had to do something to spice it up."

Something other than sleep with his wife's protégé, apparently. This guy liked things *muy caliente*. "So Chas was playing poker behind Vivienne's back."

"Oh, not just playing, honey. Chas was arranging the games. He had a regular illegal poker circuit set up."

"And you think maybe someone lost and wasn't very happy about it?"

Sadie shrugged. "Who knows? Maybe they lost. Maybe a bookie didn't like Chas taking a piece of their action. I'm not talking nickel poker here," she said, leaning in on the table again, so close her elbow bumped my coffee. "I'm talking high stakes. He invited me to a game once. I had to pass. The buy-in was three grand."

I almost choked on my latte. "Just for a seat at the table?"

Sadie nodded.

Those were high stakes indeed. "Any idea who his regular players were?" I asked.

Sadie shrugged. "Search me. I told you, I didn't buy in. I prefer to do my betting on the stock market."

I suddenly wondered if any of the big losers from Chas's games had been on my VIP list. Had another party guest seen an opportunity and slipped something into Chas's drink? Xanax was hardly difficult to come by. People in high-stress jobs like my VIPs popped it like Flintstones vitamins.

"Do you know if Chas ever took Xanax?" I asked her, switching gears.

Her eyes narrowed again. "Why? Is *that* what killed him?"

Not only was Sadie Evans not one to beat around the grapevine, but she was also a smart cookie.

I nodded, figuring the tox screen would be public knowledge soon enough. "That's what the police detective told me."

"No," she said simply. "I never saw Chas pop a Xanax."

"What about Vivienne?" I asked, wondering just who in the family might have a prescription.

"Search me," Sadie said, shrugging. She glanced at her smart watch, indicating I didn't have the money for her time much longer.

"Why did you fire Chas's sister?" I asked.

That question took her off guard. "Jenny?"

I nodded. "She said you fired her out of the blue."

Sadie let out that barking laugh again. "Well, it was hardly out of the blue, but *that* was not my call."

I frowned. "Whose was it?"

"Chas's."

That one took *me* by surprise. "Her brother? But I thought he was the one who got her the job."

Sadie shrugged. "Look, all I know is that Chas was afraid his sister suspected we were sleeping together and would tell Vivienne. He wanted me to fire her so she wouldn't have anything to go blabbing to his sugar mama about. Honestly? I thought it was a weasel move too. Like I said, the complications just weren't worth it anymore. I mean, great sex is a dime a dozen, you know?"

Sadly, I did not. I tried to remember the last great sex I'd had and came up blank.

"Anything else?" Sadie asked, glancing at her watch again.

I shook my head. "Thanks for meeting with me."

Sadie gave me a curt nod as she stood and hefted her Birkin bag onto her shoulder. "Just keep my name out of it with the press, huh? Price Digital doesn't need to be involved in this mess." The way she said it somehow implied that just because it had happened at the winery, it was *my* mess. I hoped that was not a prevailing opinion among wine lovers.

* * *

"An illegal gambling ring?" Ava yelled.

"Shhh." I glanced toward the back of the boutique. "Jenny will hear you."

Ava waved me off. "She's napping. A steady diet of tears and tea will do that to you."

I gave her a sympathetic smile. "You holding up okay?"

She nodded. "I'll live. Which is more than I can say for the underworld poker king."

I rolled my eyes. "I don't know that he was an underworld king."

As soon as Sadie had left, I'd taken my latte next door and filled Ava in on everything I'd learned, from Sadie's admission of her affair to the idea of a disgruntled high-stakes gambler and the fact that our suspect pool had just opened up to Olympic proportions.

"So, you think one of the losers at Chas's games killed him?" Ava asked.

I shrugged. "I suppose it all depends how big of a loss we're talking and how desperate his financial situation might be."

"Or hers," Ava added.

I nodded. "Right. Or hers. Sadie said the buy-in just for a seat at the table was three grand."

Ava shook her head. "I am so in the wrong business."

"Yeah, well, that business may have gotten Chas killed."

"Any idea if his players were at the winery event?"

"That's what I'd love to know," I told her, leaning my elbows on the glass case and admiring a silver necklace in a floral design. "That one new?"

Ava nodded. "I just finished it last night. You like?"

"It's gorgeous."

"Give me a week. If it doesn't sell, you can call it an early birthday present."

I shook my head. "I can't keep wearing your profits out of here."

Ava grinned at me. "I seem to remember drinking a bottle of *your* profits the other night. I owe you."

"Two weeks," I relented. "If it doesn't sell then, it can be an early birthday *and* Christmas present." What can I say? It was a really cute necklace. And I had just the top to wear it with, too.

"You think Chas had a list somewhere?" Ava said, taking the necklace out of the case so I could get a better look. "You know, of his regular players? Maybe some contact info? How much they won or lost?"

"Stands to reason he'd keep records like that," I agreed, turning the silver filigreed irises over in my hand. They were delicate yet still slightly raw on the edges, giving them an imperfect feel totally in tune with nature.

"So where would he keep something like that?" Ava asked.

I shrugged.

"Not at home," she decided. "He wouldn't want to risk Vivienne seeing it."

"But Sadie, on the other hand, already knew about the games," I said, seeing where her line of thinking was headed. "You think he kept his record at work somewhere?"

"I think it's more likely. Of course, the police have probably already confiscated all of that."

I nodded, biting my lip. "That is if they knew what to look for. To them, it might just look like a benign list of clients and figures. Without context, it would mean nothing."

Ava leaned both elbows on the glass case and cupped her chin in her hands. "We have the context. Maybe we should take a look through his records ourselves."

"And how would we do that?" I handed the necklace back to her, ashamed to say I was halfway hoping no one else had a thing for irises in the next fourteen days.

"It's not as if Price Digital is Fort Knox. They have dozens of employees who code at all hours. The main doors are never locked. Plus, Chas's office is on the sixth floor, which is mostly the marketing staff, so it's deserted at night."

I shot her a look. "How, exactly, do you know all of this?"

"I may have asked Jenny a few details about Chas's life."

"Know his shoe size too?" I mumbled, heavy on the sarcasm.

Ava cocked her head to the side and put a hand on her hip. "Hey, you want to clear your winery's name or not?"

I sighed, letting out a long breath. "Yes."

"Then it's a good thing I know the layout of Price Digital."

I felt trepidation build in my belly. "Because?"

"Because if we're going to sneak in there tonight to find Chas's secret gambling records, you're gonna need a navigator."

Oh boy.

CHAPTER TEN

Ava ordered a pizza, and I tried to choke down the cardboard consistency and make small talk with Jenny, all the while envisioning myself in prison orange for breaking and entering. Though, really, we wouldn't be breaking into anything—Ava's plan was to walk right in the front doors of Price Digital as if we had every right to be there. According to Jenny, there was no security guard on site after dark. There really wasn't much need for one, all of the company's real assets being digital. Jenny said they had a cyber security firm monitoring the company's computers for any threat or hackers 24/7. Luckily, we had no intention of digitally hacking anything—even if I'd had the slightest idea how. What we were looking for would hopefully be hiding in plain sight. Or at least plain enough for us to find before someone else found *us* snooping.

We watched a couple of Netflix shows, listened to Jenny reminisce about Chas as a kid, dried a few more of her tears. Then Ava settled her into the guest room with a story about needing to go check something at the winery with me. We both slipped out around eleven and headed to Ava's GTO—me feeling like a jittery thief and Ava's eyes shining with excitement like a kid on Christmas.

"Why do I get the feeling you're enjoying this?" I asked.

Ava grinned. "What? You can't tell me this isn't just a little bit fun playing Cagney and Lacey?"

"More like Lucy and Ethel," I mumbled.

"What was that?"

"Nothing!"

We rode the rest of the way in silence, and about an hour later pulled up in front of a sleek modern building in the Financial District of San Francisco. Ava circled the block, pulling into the underground parking garage in the rear, and I hoped that if the cameras mounted at the lift gates recorded us, no one would have a reason to check the footage for two blondes in a muscle car.

Ava led the way into the main lobby of the building, which, as she had promised, was unlocked and as well-lit as it would have been at noon, never mind that it was nearing midnight. New York might be the city that never sleeps, but San Francisco was home to the coders who hit their stride around 1:00 a.m. and seemed to need actual sunshine about as much as a vampire.

The large reception desk on the main floor was empty, but a couple of guys in jeans and hoodies stood near it, coffee cups in hands, chatting about something that was interesting enough that they barely looked up when we entered and crossed to the elevators. I felt my palms getting clammy as we rode up to the sixth floor, which was, as described, largely abandoned.

The fluorescent lights were off here, a concession to saving energy in the wee hours, though I could detect the mild hum of computers left on overnight. Our footsteps echoed eerily in the cavernous room, broken up only by rows of cubicles that hulked like dark shadows in the dim lighting. The scents of coffee and toner hung heavy in the air as Ava grabbed my arm.

"Come on," Ava said, steering me toward a row of glass-walled offices lining the back of the room. Thankfully, each was labeled with a bold black nameplate on the white lacquered doors. We passed by Sadie Evans' office—empty—and a couple of others before hitting the second to last on the row, labeled *Chas Pennington.*

I did a totally unnecessary over the shoulder, feeling guilt manifest as anxiety in my gut. Ava reached out for the door handle and turned.

Only it didn't budge.

"It's locked," she said.

"What do you mean locked?" I whispered. Totally unnecessary as well, since we were the only people I'd seen on the entire floor.

Ava shrugged. "Locked."

"I thought Jenny said the doors were unlocked at night."

"The doors to the building," Ava clarified. "I didn't ask her about Chas's private office."

Great. We'd driven all the way into the city and spiked my blood pressure a good twenty points for nothing. "So now what?" I asked.

Ava glanced around herself at the empty cubes. "Give me a minute," she said, disappearing into one.

"What are you doing?" I asked, following a step behind her.

I found her rummaging through a desk drawer, using her phone as a flashlight.

"Ava, that's someone's desk!" My gaze whipped around the room again, sure security guards were about to pop out and demand we unhand the stapler.

"Relax," she told me, closing it and opening the next one. "I'm just going to borrow something."

"What?" I asked, rubbing my sweaty palms on my jeans. I was anything *but* relaxed.

She straightened up, a look of triumph on her face. "This." She held a paperclip out.

"What is that for?"

She shot me a *well, duh* look. "To pick the lock."

I had to ask. I glanced around again, suddenly feeling extremely exposed as Ava headed back to Chas's door. I followed a step behind again, halfway hoping this failed and we could go home and halfway hoping it worked so we wouldn't be standing here in plain view of anyone who chanced to ride the elevators to the sixth floor.

Ava inserted the paperclip into the keyhole and wiggled it back and forth.

"How do you know how to pick a lock?"

"I don't," she confessed. "But this is what they did on *Castle* last week."

"Wasn't that show canceled?"

"Yes, but not because of a lack of realistic PI skills," she told me sagely.

I barely resisted the urge to roll my eyes. Okay, maybe I didn't resist. But in the dark, I didn't think Ava saw me.

"I saw that," she mumbled, the tip of her tongue poking out the corner of her mouth as she concentrated on the lock.

"Are you sure about this?" I asked. "What if we get caught? What if the cameras are watching? What if we damage the door?'

"Geez, you're tightly wound."

I shot her a look. "Only when committing minor felonies."

Ava's turn to roll her eyes. "Calm down, will you? This is misdemeanor at best."

I opened my mouth to tell her there was nothing "at best" about a misdemeanor, when I heard a soft click and the doorknob in her hand turned.

Ava looked about as surprised as I felt, her eyes going from me to the door. "Huh. It worked."

"Let's go, *Cagney*," I said, ushering her inside as quickly as I could. The less time we stood out on the open floor, the better.

With the door safely closed behind us, Ava flipped on the light, and I took a moment to survey the surroundings. One thing I could say, Chas hadn't skimped on his office amenities. While he might not have done much more than be a pretty face to brighten Vivienne's workday, his office was well appointed with everything the wealthy and pretending-to-work could want. A full bar sat along one wall, under framed photos of Chas golfing, skiing, yachting, and generally enjoying the spoils of his wife's labor. An oversized wooden desk sat on the opposite wall, the top of it cleared of any papers and gleaming as if seldom used. A pair of file cabinets sat behind it, along with a bookshelf that housed several leather-bound volumes, none looking as if they were ever read. A large leather chair sat behind the desk, which faced a window overlooking the twinkling lights of the city.

Beside the bar was a long, low sofa, which was the one thing in the room that looked like it *had* gotten plenty of use, the cushions indented in all the right places. I wondered if Sadie was the only woman Chas had been *getting caught up with* at work.

I noticed several wires coming out of the wall and empty shelving to the right of the desk, where electronics might have sat. Grant had already been there and had taken the computer with him. The detective was thorough.

"Let's hope Chas was old school when it came to record keeping," Ava said, her gaze landing on the same empty spot in the room that mine had.

I nodded. "You take the filing cabinets. I'll take the desk."

Ava started on the paper files, working in total silence, while I looked through the desk drawers. Nothing much there, apart from the usual office flotsam, a couple sticks of gum, and an old copy of *Playboy.* Ick.

"Anything?" I asked Ava, starting to feel antsy. I wasn't sure how long we'd been in Chas's office, but it felt like an eternity, each minute that ticked by pushing us one step closer to being found.

Ava shook her head. "Mostly old accounting files. Lots of expense receipts."

I moved beside her to look at some. She wasn't kidding when she said there were a lot. Chas had expensed everything from Cuban cigars to $400 sneakers to company accounts. Not only was Chas running through Vivienne's funds, but he was apparently playing fast and loose with corporate ones as well. I wondered if Vivienne knew. Or Sadie, for that matter. Maybe she hadn't so much tired of her Greek god's complications as his spending habits.

"I'll look through the bookcase," Ava said, leaving me with the receipts.

I browsed through several more files, finding my opinion of Chas going downhill with each one. If Chas did anything at Price Digital other than spend money, it wasn't evident in his files. In fact, what was evident was that someone in accounting had begun to notice the spending too. I found several expense reimbursement requests marked as *denied.* Someone had been tightening the purse strings.

"Whoa."

I looked up to find Ava holding one of the leather-bound books in her hands.

"What?" I asked.

"I found Chas's secret stash."

I crossed the room to look at the book she was holding. Though, upon closer inspection, it wasn't a useable book at all. Someone had hollowed it out, creating a hiding space inside. One that was filled with a small baggie of white powder.

I blinked at it. "What is that?"

Ava shrugged. "I'm guessing it's not baby powder."

"Cocaine?"

"No idea." She moved to pick up the baggie.

"Wait!" I put a hand on her arm to stop her.

She froze.

"Don't get your prints on it."

Ava carefully closed the book back up and wiped the cover of it with the hem of her shirt.

"If Grant didn't find this the first time, we don't want our prints on it when he comes back."

She nodded and slowly put the book back on the shelf. I noticed the title on the spine: *The Call of the Wild.* Chas had had a sense of humor.

An idea struck me, and I looked over the other titles on the shelf, my eyes falling on a copy of *The Black Sheep.*

I pulled the sleeve of my shirt over my hand and reached for the book. I gingerly opened it…

Bingo.

It, too, was hollowed out. And inside was a small black notebook.

Ava's eyes lit up. "Is that what I think it is?'

I pulled the notebook out, hands still wrapped in my sleeve, and flipped through the pages. Dates. Initials. Dollar amounts. "I think it is."

Ava did a little victory dance, lifting her feet up and down in a jogging motion. "Ohmigod, we actually found it!"

While I was dancing with her on the inside, I still felt like we were on borrowed time. I quickly flipped to the last couple of pages. Dates from the last three months. No names, unfortunately, just initials. But it was a start. I pulled my phone out and took a photo, hoping to compare the initials to our guest list from the Spanish party.

I thumbed back through the last six months' worth of dates, skimming the pages. There seemed to be at least four entries for every date—which I assumed corresponded to the players at each of Chas's games. The sums were staggering, some ranging in the five figures. It was hard to tell exactly what they corresponded to—winnings or losings—but I took photos of several more pages, hoping to figure out Chas's system in the privacy and safety of Ava's loft later.

I was just photographing the last page, when one of the sets of initials caught my eyes. D.A. While it could have stood for almost anything, I immediately thought of the name David Allen. I scrolled back further, checking for any other entries. For almost every date of a game, there was some entry for D.A. I felt my stomach lifting, puzzle pieces falling into place. David Allen had not only known about his stepfather's illegal poker games, but he'd also been gambling at them. Maybe losing? I checked the last entry for the D.A. initials. The dollar amount listed next to it was thirty grand.

Was David losing enough to kill over?

I opened my mouth to tell Ava, but before I could do more than call her name, I heard the ping of the elevators.

Instinctively, I ducked down to the floor, using Chas's large desk as a shield. Ava did the same, dropping to the carpeted floor.

"I thought you said there were no security guards," I whispered to her.

Ava shrugged. "Jenny said there weren't."

I dared to peek around the corner of the wooden drawers as a flashlight beam cut through the darkness. I ducked back behind the desk, waiting until the beam swept to the other side of the sixth floor, to peek out again to get a look at the shadowed figure holding it. While the dim light made it difficult to make out facial features, I'd know those unmistakable black boots, tight jeans, and broad shoulders anywhere.

Detective Christopher Grant.

CHAPTER ELEVEN

I thought a really dirty word, ducking back down behind the desk again as the flashlight beam made another sweep our way. I wasn't sure what he was looking for, but I knew what I didn't want him to find…two snooping blondes.

"Is that who I think it is?" Ava whispered to me, peering out from behind the file cabinets where she'd taken refuge.

I nodded. "Detective Grant."

I wondered if Grant was investigating suspects beyond Jenny, or if he was only here to find evidence to support his disgruntled former-employee/sister as the killer theory.

"What do we do now?" I whispered, hearing the soft fall of footsteps as Grant moved around the floor.

"Confess and ask for mercy?" Ava asked.

I snorted. "Clearly you don't know Grant as well as I do."

That earned me a raised eyebrow and a smirk from my friend.

"Not like that," I said, waving her off. "He's just not the mercy type."

"Agreed," she whispered. "So plan B?"

I peeked out the glass wall, scanning the room for any escape routes. Unfortunately, Grant was still standing directly in front of the elevators. To our right was what looked like a small break room. To the left, a restroom.

"There," I decided. I crossed my fingers, hoping that Grant hadn't brought any female officers who'd had one too many coffees this shift.

I still had the little black book in my hand, but I didn't dare risk standing erect to put it back on the shelf. Instead, I shoved it under the desk, hoping my sleeve did the trick to obliterate any prints. I glanced out the glass wall again, waiting until Grant's attention was focused on the other side of the room. Then I quickly opened the office door and duck-walked beneath the short cube walls as fast as I could in three-inch heels toward the ladies' room, Ava a waddling step behind me.

Out of the corner of my eye, I saw Grant's flashlight beam cut across the room toward Chas's office, his shadowy figure following it in that direction. But I didn't wait to see more, quickly slipping into the ladies' room.

As soon as the door shut silently behind us, Ava and I leaned against its safety. My breath suddenly seemed loud enough to echo off the walls, coming out in a ragged pant that matched my best friend's.

"That was close," Ava mumbled.

I nodded. I could hear footsteps outside the door, drawing closer to Chas's office. "What do you think he's doing here?"

Ava shrugged. "Same thing we are?"

I wondered. Had Grant found out about the illegal poker games too? Maybe the detective deserved more credit than I'd previously given him.

We waited and listened, though once we heard the sound of Chas's office door opening and shutting there wasn't a whole lot more to be heard. Whatever Grant was doing in there was too muffled to pinpoint. We waited some more. Then some more. Then more, until we got so tired of standing, we sat down in stalls next to each other, with the doors open. Then we waited some more. After a further hour by my watch, I opened the restroom door a crack to survey the sixth floor. I strained to hear anything, but all that came back was the steady hum of computer equipment. No light shone from Chas's office. No sign of life anywhere.

"Is he gone?" Ava whispered at my back.

I nodded. "I think so."

Gingerly we exited the ladies' room and did a tiptoe run toward the elevator doors. I let out a sigh of relief as they closed, hugging us into the relative safety of the brightly lit carriage.

Ava leaned her head backward against the elevator wall, and I could see the anxiety draining off her as well.

"Think Cagney and Lacey ever got stuck hiding in a restroom?" I joked.

Ava smirked. "Alright, I give up. We're totally Lucy and Ethel."

I chuckled as the elevator doors slid open at the lobby, and we power walked as nonchalantly as we could back toward the parking garage and Ava's 1970s getaway car.

* * *

Possibly due to a guilty conscience over our near miss with the law, Ava drove just under the speed limit the entire way back to Sonoma, which added a good half hour onto our return trip. By the time she dropped me off at my car, and I'd made the trip to the top of the Oak Valley driveway, I was exhausted, drained, and could think of nothing more wonderful than the big, fluffy white comforter on my bed, beckoning me like a pillowy beacon.

Unfortunately, as I pulled my keys from my purse and approached the door to my cottage, there was just one obstacle between me and said fluffy comforter. And he stood about six feet in black boots and tight jeans.

I licked my lips. "Uh, Detective Grant?" I asked.

His broad shoulders leaned against my doorframe in a casual posture that said he'd been waiting awhile. "Late night?" he asked.

Instinctively I glanced at my watch. It was past two. "Uh, yeah. I, uh, had a date," I lied.

One eyebrow rose. "Really?"

I mentally crossed my fingers behind my back as I nodded. "Yep. A really nice date."

"Went kind of late, huh?"

I put one hand on my hip, trying at indignant. "What exactly are you implying?"

Grant shook his head. "Nothing. Your private life is none of my business."

"Darn right it's not." Though something about the whole conversation was making me distinctly uncomfortable. And not just the fact that I was fibbing so hard I expected my nose to grow like a birch branch from my face. "Exactly what are you doing here?" I asked, crossing both arms over my chest.

"New evidence has come to light, and I wanted to ask you some questions."

"At two in the morning?" I challenged.

A challenge he ignored, going on as smoothly as silk. "There was a break-in this evening at Price Digital."

My heart froze. In fact, my entire body froze even as my brain when into overdrive, quickly trying to anticipate what he'd say next and to come up with an appropriate lie to cover it.

"Oh?" I said, with what I hoped was enough surprise to sound genuine.

"You don't sound too surprised."

Drat. I was a really lousy liar.

I shrugged. "They're a big company. Lots of competitors. I imagine break-ins happen all the time."

Grant nodded. "I suppose that could be true."

"How do you know someone broke in?" I asked, praying we hadn't left a trail of evidence.

"A silent alarm was tripped on the sixth floor."

I thought my second R-rated word of the night. Jenny hadn't mentioned anything about a silent alarm system. Though, it's possible she hadn't known anything about it.

"Anything taken?" I asked, fishing for what he knew.

He took a beat to answer, slowly shaking his head. "No, but items were disturbed. It looked like we caught the thieves in progress."

If he only knew.

"Well, nothing taken. No harm done, right?" I said, hoping to gloss over it all.

Though that hope was probably in vain. Grant's eyes hadn't left my face since the whole date comment. Probably waiting for any sign of guilt. They were staring me down as if the longer they looked, the deeper into my psyche they could see. I watched the little gold flecks dancing, almost hypnotizing me.

"You don't happen to know why someone would be looking through Chas Pennington's office, do you?"

"Me?" I squeaked out, my voice high enough to audition for a role in the next *Chipmunks* movie. I cleared my throat. "Uh, no. I mean, why would I?"

Grant shrugged. "You seem awfully close to this case."

"Do I?" I asked on a shaky breath.

He nodded. "Friends with Jenny. Wooing Mrs. Price-Pennington as a client. Not to mention that your winery was the scene of the crime."

"You're not blaming *me* for someone killing Chas at my winery, are you?"

"No," he said slowly. "But I'd like to think you aren't withholding any information from the authorities."

I'd like him to think that too.

"Look, I have no idea who killed Chas Pennington"—sadly, totally true—"but I know it wasn't Jenny"—okay, I was 90% sureish—"and I have total faith that you'll find whoever did." I was 50/50 on that one. But I hoped he'd take to the flattery.

"Oh, I will," he promised. Though instead of sounding flattered, the comment came out more like a threat. I suddenly felt a teensy bit sorry for whoever had murdered Chas. The wrath of Grant was not something I ever wanted to experience.

He took a step away from the door, no longer blocking my entry. "But until I do catch the perpetrator, I'd appreciate it if you stayed away from the Price-Penningtons." He added, "And Price Digital."

I swallowed. "Of course. Why would I have any reason to be at Price Digital?"

He pinned me with a hard look. "I wonder."

I waited for the interrogation to follow, but instead he left it at that, turning toward the paved walkway to the drive without another word.

I watched until the darkness swallowed him up before moving to unlock my door. My hands were shaking, making my keys jingle in the silence as I pushed inside. It wasn't until I heard the sound of a car engine start up and fade toward the main road that I felt I could breathe again.

CHAPTER TWELVE

I tossed and turned for a few hours, my body refusing to fall into a deep sleep. I wondered if this was how criminals felt—guilt, fear, and nerves keeping my mind way too active to rest. I finally fell asleep in the early hours of the morning, though I was awakened shortly after by the sound of my phone ringing from my nightstand.

I fumbled for it, only conceding to open one eye to check the readout. But as soon as I saw who the caller was, I bolted awake.

"Mom? What's wrong? Are you okay?"

"Good morning, honey," came my mother's voice on the other end of the phone. "Goodness, nothing's wrong. You're such a worrier."

The adrenaline that had shot through me at seeing her name subsided some. I glanced at the clock hanging above my dresser. 7:15.

"It's early, Mom," I told her.

"Is it? I'm sorry. I've been up for hours."

I yawned, leaning my head back into the pillows. "It's fine," I told her. "I was awake anyway." Hey, I was already going to hell for lying to Grant—I might as well throw a comfort lie in there for Mom too.

"Good. Listen, I wanted to know what you want for your birthday, Emmy?"

"My birthday?"

"Uh-huh. It's coming up, you know."

"Mom, my birthday is in December. It's barely summer."

"Oh." I heard disappointment in my mother's voice. "Is it? I could have sworn it was coming up. I must have lost track of time."

I bit my lip, that sinking weight that often accompanied chats with my mom filling my belly. It was the desperation of losing something you dearly wanted to hold on to and knowing it was totally futile to try.

"It's okay," I told her softly, trying to keep that weight out of my voice. "It's never too early to plan for a birthday, right?"

"I agree," she said, her voice perking up a bit.

"But what I'd really love is one of your apple strudels," I told her.

"Oh, I remember how you used to love those." Mom laughed. "When you were a girl, I had to hide them while they cooled. Otherwise, they'd always be missing a piece."

I grinned at the memory. "Well, I tell you what? For my birthday I'll pick you up and we'll come bake apple strudels together at the winery. Sound good?"

"That sounds lovely."

"It's a date then," I told her, only feeling a little sad that the date was months away. Then again, summer felt like a lovely time for strudel too.

I hung up after giving my mom some heartfelt I-love-you's and promising to come visit her later this week. Though I had no idea if she'd remember the promise or even what week it was.

I shoved that thought down as I got up, showered, and tried to trick my body into thinking I'd had a real night's sleep with a full pot of extra dark coffee. Conchita and Hector had the day off, and I took my third cup into my office with me, checking the emails from our website account.

One from a company promising to optimize our SEO. Three inquiries from journalists and bloggers hoping to get a quote from the owner of the "killer vineyard." And, I realized with a sinking heart, two event cancelations. One a corporate retreat for a streaming site, which had been booked three months in advance, and the other a private anniversary party for a couple who'd frequented the winery in my parents' day. The coffee stung my empty stomach as I calculated how these losses would affect our bottom line this month. Suffice to say, it was not good. Shultz would no longer so much have a seesaw as a lead weight in one hand.

I closed my computer, all of it too depressing, and went into the main kitchen to indulge in some much-needed cooking therapy. Plus, I was starving. And since it was that kind of week, I went for chocolate. I pulled out my mother's recipe for Espresso Waffles with Mocha Sauce—one of my favorites when we used to have Sunday brunches together.

I carefully measured out flour, cocoa powder, and baking powder and soda in equal amounts, before adding in milk, eggs, and butter. Once the batter was gooey, I set the waffle iron to heat and created the signature Mocha Syrup from sweetened condensed milk, strong coffee, and melted dark chocolate—maybe sampling a few nibbles of the chocolate as I cooked.

Once the waffles were crispy and the sauce gooey, I garnished them with raspberries and toasted almonds before digging in.

As I devoured generous forkfuls of the chocolaty heaven on a plate, I picked up my phone and pulled up the photos I'd taken of Chas Pennington's little black book the previous evening. I scrolled through, taking note of the initials next to each date. Several were repeated, as one would expect from repeat players, but none with the frequency of D.A. While it was possible the initials could have belonged to someone else, I'd bet anything it was David Allen. I thought back to how honest he'd been about his dislike of Chas. I'd taken it for a defiant attitude at the time, but now I wondered if he'd played at open hatred of his stepfather to throw me off the real relationships he'd had with Chas—that of gambler and beneficiary. If David had been losing, maybe he figured it was easier to off his stepfather than make good on the debts. Or, maybe Chas had threatened to tell Vivienne that David was gambling, and David had feared being cut off from his mother's purse strings. Either way, it made for a fantastic motive for David Allen.

If it were true.

I had a lot of best-guesswork here but little evidence. And I couldn't ignore the other names on the list. While David's seemed to show up with the most frequency, I had to admit that other initials lay next to the highest dollar amounts. A P.T., for example, had been in for five figures just three weeks ago. I wondered if he'd made good on the debt or if it was still outstanding.

I scrolled for a few more minutes until Ava's number popped up with a text.

You up?

I shot back, *Unfortunately.*

A beat later my phone rang, Ava's face filling the screen. I swiped it on.

"Hey," I said by way of greeting.

"Couldn't sleep either?" she asked.

I shook my head, even though I knew she couldn't see me. "No. But I have coffee, so I'll live."

"Lucky. Half Calf doesn't open for another thirty minutes."

I grinned. Ava had a serious latte addiction. I'd tried to duplicate her favorite coffee shop's syrupy, foamy concoctions with the cappuccino maker I'd given her for Christmas last year, but she still held out for the real deal from the place next door every morning. A hardship when they opened late midweek.

"What are you up to?" she asked.

"Just browsing the photos we took last night."

"In Chas's office?"

"Shhh!" I admonished automatically

Ava's laugh tickled across the line. "It's not like Grant has your phone tapped."

I wouldn't put it past him.

"He was here, waiting for me to get home last night."

Ava sucked in a breath on the other end. "Uh-oh. I can't imagine that went well."

"No," I confessed. "It did not."

I quickly filled Ava in on the conversation we'd had, the fact that I was pretty sure Grant knew, or at least suspected, we'd been the ones to trip the silent alarm at Price Digital, and the fruits of our in-the-gray-area-of-legal search of Chas's office—namely the contents of his little black book.

"How often did he run the games?" Ava asked.

I scrolled through photos as I answered. "Looks like there's a new entry roughly every week or so. Sometimes more often."

"I wonder how he found these players," Ava mused.

"What do you mean?'

"Well, it isn't as if you can openly advertise an illegal poker game, right?"

I nodded. She had a good point. "If we knew where he found his players, maybe we could identify some of them." While my mind immediately went to David Allen, I tried to think where else Chas might meet wealthy, idle people with time and money to burn.

And one place practically leapt to mind.

"What about the Sonoma Links?" I asked.

"The golf club?" Ava asked.

While Sonoma had a country club proper, anyone who was anyone was a member at the Links—whether they golfed or just enjoyed the above-the-fray gossip over bloody marys in the lounge and margaritas on the terrace. "You think that's where Chas found his players?"

"We know he was a member. And it's the right crowd."

"Yeah, but would any of them cop to knowledge of the games now?"

"I don't know," I mused. "But I'd love to ask around." I paused. "I don't suppose you know any members who could get us in?"

"As a matter of fact, I do," she said, brightening on the other end to almost as chipper as the post-caffeine Ava I knew and loved. "I know him quite well in fact."

* * *

We made plans to meet for lunch at the Links, and I spent the rest of the morning cleaning up the kitchen, doing laundry, tidying up my cottage, and generally trying not to think about the impending doom of my winery failing, Grant suspecting me of minor B&E, and the murderer on the loose. Since the breakfast had lifted my spirits a bit, I decided to make a trip into town to pick up a few things for dinner as well. If life kept at it this way, I might have to go with a one-piece bathing suit this season.

By noon, I was ensconced in a long-sleeved T-shirt style dress in a bold floral pattern that felt right for spring at an exclusive club. I tossed on a couple of silver bangles Ava had made for me last year, and capped it off with a pair of silver wedge sandals. Then I grabbed my bag and hopped into my Jeep.

Midday sunlight warmed the rolling hills of pale greens, yellows, and the deep emerald of the new buds growing in rowed patterns. Even the bare patches that were still darkened with the remnants of crops before the fires were starting to grow back, with sparse patches of green struggling to push through the wet earth, proving that Mother Nature never missed an opportunity for a comeback.

It was a short drive to the gated entrance of the Links, where I gave my name as the guest of one Ken Barnett—Ava's father, who, as she had told me earlier, had been an active member of the club since before it was chic to be so.

I followed the winding drive up a hill much like the one to my own Oak Valley Vineyards. Only, while mine was lined with natural growth oaks, a gravel drive, and wildflowers, the one at Links sported tall, manicured cypress trees, sprawling green lawns, and colorful nonnative annuals in bright blues, pinks, and reds that looked both delicate and abundant.

A valet took my car, and I stepped into the club feeling only a little self-conscious—as if my bank account balance was apparent in my attire. The outfit had looked simple and elegant at home, but here I felt as if every eye could see its lack of designer label.

"Emmy!" Thankfully, Ava hailed me from a table in the lounge almost as soon as I stepped inside. Her friendly smile and upbeat aura eased my tension a little as I air kissed her and sat at the table for three.

"Nice to see you again, Emmy," Mr. Barnett told me, shaking my hand.

"You too. Thanks for the invite for lunch."

"Well, anytime Ava makes time for Dad, I try to accommodate." He grinned at his daughter, the genuine affection hard to miss. I felt a twinge in my chest, wishing my own father was still around to chide me for not making enough time for him.

Ava and I both ordered Caesar salads with chilled avocado-cucumber soup and Chardonnay, while Ken went for a cocoa-rubbed filet and a cabernet. We made polite chitchat as the food arrived, Ken regaling me with some embarrassing stories from Ava's childhood I'd yet to hear, and Ava giving her dad updates on the shop. I zoned out a bit when talk turned to one of her cousins who was getting married that fall, my attention falling on the food that, for all intents and purposes, was my competition. It was undeniably delicious, with attention to details that made the meal. But there was also an overarching sense of desperation to impress both in the seasonings and the presentation. Pretty, elegant, but lacking heart. I could do better. If my balance sheets were any indications, I *had* to do better.

"…were so sorry to hear about the trouble at the winery."

I realized that Ken was talking to me and pulled my attention back to our host.

"I can't believe someone died at your party, Emmy."

I forced a smile I didn't feel. "Thanks, but the police are looking into it. They're confident they'll find the perpetrator soon," I told him, repeating the promise Grant had given me the night before.

"I actually saw Vivienne earlier. She's planning to have the memorial here," he went on. "Of course, only fitting. The club is the only suitable location. Bud Cassidy's memorial in January was quite impressive. The lounge was packed."

Ava cleared her throat, throwing me a meaningful glance out of the corner of her eyes before addressing her father. "Uh, did you know Chas Pennington, Daddy?" she asked.

"Oh well, I saw him here often, of course. Might have shaken hands with him at a party or two, but I can't say I knew him well."

"What about his stepson, David Allen?" I asked, jumping on the opening.

He nodded. "Yes, he's a member too." He frowned.

I had a feeling David Allen wasn't quite up to Ken Barnett's standards as far as members went.

"Was he here often?" I asked, thinking the indie club scene felt more like David's thing than the golf club set.

"Oh, not often. He came with his mother most weekends for brunch, but that was it. His grandmother accompanied them too. If I had to guess, he came under duress, but one could say that about ninety percent of the men accompanying the ladies to Sunday brunch." He gave me a knowing wink.

"Did Chas come too?" I asked.

Ken frowned and shook his head. "No, not that I can recall. But Chas and Viv sort of did their own thing, as far as I could tell. Chas liked to golf, but I don't ever recall seeing him and Viv on the links together."

"Vivienne didn't golf?" I asked.

Ken nodded, his soft jowls wavering with aftershocks. "Oh, she golfs alright. In fact, she was a very active member of several committees when the Pacific Coast tour came through here last fall."

"You were on that committee too, right, Daddy?" Ava prompted.

He nodded again, and Ava and I waited for him to continue as he sipped his drink. "I was. Vivienne could be quite demanding, but sometimes you need that. Point her in the right direction, and she gets things done. And she's not a bad golfer either. Her drive is pretty good, but she's too impulsive to putt well."

That fit with what I knew of Vivienne so far. "It doesn't sound as if she and her husband shared many activities. Any idea what their relationship was like?" I asked.

But Ken clearly wasn't the type to gossip, simply shrugging. "They seemed to get along fine," was all he said.

"What else did Chas like to do?" Ava pressed, giving me the side-eye again. "Was he a gambler, by chance?"

"Well, I don't know about all that." He paused, his gaze going across the room. "Robby!"

A dark-haired man sipping a midday scotch at the bar turned toward our table. Ken hailed him over, and as he approached, said, "Robby used to make up a foursome with Chas on the weekends. He'd know him better."

"Hey, Kenny." Robby nodded to Ava's dad. "And who are these lovely ladies?" His eyes went from Ava to me and back to Ava's cleavage.

"This is Ava. My *daughter*," Ken emphasized.

Robby's eyes shot back up into a respectable zone, his smile going from eager to mildly pleasant.

"And this is her friend, Emmy. Emmy owns the Oak Valley Vineyards."

"Robby Bettencourt." He shoved a warm palm my way, shaking in greeting. "You're young to own a winery."

"It's my family's," I explained, trying to tamp down the discomfort at how long Robby was holding on to my hand.

"Well, I'll have to come check it out sometime."

"I hope you do." I gave him a big smile as I extracted my fingers from his sweaty grip.

"Uh, we hear that you played golf with Chas Pennington," Ava said, thankfully getting right to the point.

Robby pulled an empty chair up next to her and nodded, his expression going somber at the mention of the dead man. "I did. He had a 10 handicap, but he landed an eagle on the 18th the other day. And that's a par 5 hole."

I had no idea what that meant, but by the way Ken nodded appreciatively, I figured it was good.

"We were wondering, did Chas ever mention any poker games to you?" Ava asked.

Robby's eyes cut from Ava to me. "Poker?"

"We, uh, heard from a mutual friend that he used to organize games. You know, for fun," I said, trying to make light of the situation in hopes he'd open up.

But his expression remained as unreadable as if he'd been holding a full house. "I don't know anything about that," he said.

Ava pouted, making full use of her plump lips and Revlon's Racing Red color that she'd applied liberally. "Oh, that's a shame. They sounded fun."

"You play?" Robby asked, his eyes cutting to Ken. I could tell he wanted to ask more but was treading on thin ice with Dad there.

"Uh, Mr. Barnett, would you mind terribly getting me another glass of Chardonnay?" I asked, lifting my empty one his way with a sunny smile.

If he thought anything of it, he didn't mention it, saying, "Of course. Anyone else need a refill?"

Ava quickly knocked back the contents of her glass and handed the empty to her dad with the same sort of innocent smile I was sure *I* was not faking well.

As soon as he stepped away from the table, Ava leaned in to Robby. "Listen, you and I both know that it's not just a rumor that there's a regular underground poker game. I'd love to get in on that if I could." She batted her eyelashes at him in the way only a well-endowed twentysomething could get away with.

And it had the desired effect.

Robby's face broke into a salacious smile, eyes going to Ava's chest again. "I knew there was a bit of bad girl in you."

Ava ginned at him, flirting for all she was worth.

"Unfortunately, I'm not sure there will be any more games," he informed us.

"So, Chas was running the games?" I asked.

Robby tore his eyes way from Ava's cleavage with some difficulty, focusing on me for a second. "Yes, he organized the odd game here and there."

"And you played?" I asked, trying to recall if a R.B. had shown up in Chas's little black book.

Robby shrugged. "I may have. But these were just social games. Purely for fun," he added with a big grin.

Yeah right. With a three grand buy-in, these were not "for fun" games. But I played along. "Do you happen to know who else might have been at these social games?"

Robby's eyes narrowed ever so slightly. "Why do you want to know?"

"Uh…"

"Uh, the truth is," Ava jumped in, "we were thinking of organizing a little game of fun of our own. Only, we're not members here." She pouted again.

"Now, that is a crying shame." Back was the salacious grin. This guy had #metoo oozing from his slimy pores.

"So we don't exactly know who to ask. You know, people who can be discreet," I hinted.

"And fun," Ava said, giving Robby a wink.

I think it was the wink that did it. Robby melted right into her sunny charms. "Well, I'm not sure I could give you a definitive list. I think you'd have to ask David for that."

"That would be David Allen?" I asked in what I hoped wasn't too eager of a voice.

Robby nodded. "He was at almost all of Chas's games."

That much I knew.

"He must have owed Chas a good deal," I fished.

Only to my surprise, Robby shook his head. "On the contrary. David had an uncanny knack for coming out ahead."

I cocked my head to the side. "Are you sure?" All the figures I'd seen beside his initials seemed to be large enough to dispute that fact.

But Robby nodded. "Kicked my behind, I'll tell you. Kid had a gift. If I didn't know better, I'd say he was counting cards or something. I told Chas as much, but he laughed me off. Just said the kid had a lot of time on his hands. Watched YouTube videos on how to play poker or something."

I was about to ask more, when Ava's dad picked that moment to return to the table, drinks in hand.

"Two Chardonnays?" he asked.

We each thanked him in turn and took our glasses. Robby took that as his cue to depart, though not before telling Ava, "Let me know if you decide to put together a, uh…game night." He punctuated the statement with a knowing wink.

Ava batted her eyelashes at him, but as soon as he had his back turned on his way toward the bar, she made a mock gagging motion.

"Ava!" her dad chided.

"Sorry." She put a hand on Ken's arm. "But if you ever make eyes at a woman half your age, I'm gonna make gagging faces at you too."

Ken grinned, showing off a dimple in his weathered cheek that matched his daughter's. "If I ever did that, your mother would put me six feet under. Then dance on my grave."

Ava laughed out loud. "Too true."

We finished our meal, and I excused myself to stroll around the grounds as Ava and her dad caught up a bit more. Ostensibly, it was to take in the air, but the truth was the second glass of distraction Chardonnay had hit me hard enough that I knew I needed a walk and some fresh air.

I left the lounge by way of the French doors at the back and wound my way around the massive terrace that overlooked the golf course. I had to admit, I'd only played a few times myself, but the soft carpet of thick green lawn stretching as far as the eye could see had a calming effect, even if I didn't have a club in my hand.

As I strolled, I waved to a couple of people I recognized from my Spanish party, making mental notes to check their initials against my little black book later. Then instantly felt guilty about thinking of every one of my party guests as a potential suspect. I was not a suspicious person by nature, and it wasn't sitting well with me now.

I left the terrace, heading down a small flight of wooden stairs to the ground level, and found a shady spot under a group of trees on the back side of the pro shop. I leaned against the wood siding of the shop, inhaling the sweet scents of pine trees, freshly mowed grass, and a hint of meat being smoked in the kitchen.

It might have been a serene moment, had it not been interrupted by raised voices just on the other side of the building.

My first instinct was to walk away and let the couple argue in private. But I stopped as I recognized one of them. The deep, throaty, and commanding voice of Vivienne Price-Pennington.

Hadn't Ken said he'd seen her at the club making memorial arrangements earlier? I ducked my head around the corner to confirm my suspicions. It was Vivienne alright, decked out in head-to-toe black in a pressed pantsuit that looked uncomfortably out of place in the warm California weather. But whatever she was discussing now, it was not subdued flower arrangements and eulogies. She was deep in a discussion with a stocky man in a cheap suit. Her eyebrows were drawn, her hands gesturing wildly in the air, and I could see by the strain in her posture that this was not a friendly chat.

I leaned forward, halfway hating myself for eavesdropping and halfway wanting to inch closer to better make out what she was saying.

"...how dare you... know who I am... not fair, Trask..."

Vivienne was angry about something, that was for sure. What, I couldn't tell, hearing only snippets of her tirade.

The man—presumably Trask—had a lower voice, much deeper, that came out as a mumbled rumble from my vantage point.

"...don't care where you get it...the last time I agree to this...or else..."

I blinked, the meaning of his words hitting me. *Or else.*

Vivienne Price-Pennington was being threatened.

CHAPTER THIRTEEN

I took a step closer to the pair, flattening myself against the pro shop building as cover, and strained to hear more. But the threat must have had the intended effect, as Vivienne lowered her voice, and I couldn't make out anything other than a murmur.

I edged closer to the corner to get a better look at the guy who dared threaten Price-Pennington royalty. I quietly slunk around the side of the building…

And almost ran straight into Trask.

He sidestepped me just in time, giving me a deep scowl. "Watch it," he warned. His bushy eyebrows drew down over a pair of dark eyes. A nose that looked a size too big for his face sat above a mouth that was creased with lines on both sides, giving it a downward turn that was intensified by the surly look on his face.

"Sorry," I mumbled, quickly backtracking toward the clubhouse before Vivienne caught me. Something in the stocky guy's demeanor—not to mention the way he'd threatened Vivienne—spelled danger, and I didn't want to be anywhere on his radar.

As I trekked back up the wooden staircase, I wondered just what the argument could have been about. Possibly Chas? Had Trask had something to do with his death, and Vivienne found out? The guy looked like he could have fit right into any gangster movie. All he needed was an Al Pacino accent and I'd believe he was hiding a "little friend" in his coat.

Of course, if Vivienne had found out he'd been involved in Chas's death, wouldn't she be the one threatening him—not the other way around? Could it be that *Vivienne* had actually had something to do with her husband's demise, and the gangster looking Trask was threatening *her* about it? Possibly with blackmail?

I had just reached the end of the terrace, when I spotted another member of the Price-Pennington royal family at a table overlooking the 9th hole—Alison Price.

Alison Price hid under a wide-brimmed white hat, wearing matching white blouse and slacks—no black mourning attire for her. She sipped a glass of rosé and glanced up as I approached. At first, I'd swear she didn't recognize me, her face a complete blank. But as I waved, her mouth strained to curve into a small smile, and she nodded her hat in my direction.

"Emmeline Oak, yes?" she said as I approached her table.

I nodded. "Please, call me Emmy."

She forced a smile again but didn't amend her previous moniker. "I didn't realize you were a member here?"

"I'm not," I confessed.

"Oh?" It was phrased as a question, but I had a feeling she was well aware of my membership status already.

"I was here having lunch with a member. Ken Barnett."

"Ah." She nodded, sipping her rosé. "Yes, I know Ken. Mediocre golfer but a pillar of the community."

I wasn't sure Ken wouldn't rather be a referred to as a great golfer and mediocre pillar, but I nodded and smiled anyway. "How are you holding up?" I asked.

She blinked at me as if trying to recall what I could possibly be talking about.

"I'm sure Chas's passing has been hard on all of you."

"Oh. Yes. That tragedy." She sipped her drink again, neither confirming nor denying my assumption.

"I, uh, saw Vivienne just now," I ventured, watching her reaction.

"Yes. She's making arrangements."

"I noticed her chatting with someone. A man named Trask. Do you happen to know who he is?" I asked.

Alison frowned at me "Name doesn't ring a bell. But there are so many new members here. They're getting lax with the requirements these days."

I had a feeling whatever Vivienne's argument with the stocky man had been about, Mother was blissfully unaware. Of course, if I had killed my husband, I wouldn't go bragging to my mom either.

"I met one of Chas's golf buddies earlier," I said, changing the subject. "It seems Chas was very popular here at the club."

Alison let out a short bark of laughter. "Yes, well, I'm sure he was popular wherever he went. He was good at that." She sipped at her glass again. Though, this time the sip might have veered into gulp territory, which emboldened me to ask my next question.

"Say, you wouldn't happen to know if your grandson, David, has a prescription for Xanax, would you?"

She frowned into her wineglass. "Yes. David has anxiety. I believe the Xanax helps."

I felt my heart speed up. David had motive, opportunity, and now it turned out ample means to the murder weapon.

My excitement at a solid lead must have shown on my face, as Alison lifted her eyes to meet mine, squinting up at me. "Why do you ask?"

"Oh, uh, no reason," I lied. "I just…he seemed jittery last we spoke. Glad he's finding some relief. Well, please give my best to Vivienne," I said, edging away from the suspicion in her eyes before she could ask anything more.

But Alison put up a finger, beckoning me to wait as she set her glass down on the tabletop. "Speaking of Chas's untimely demise," she began.

Uh-oh.

"Vivienne is making arrangements to have the memorial here on Thursday," she continued. "Perhaps you'd be free to cater the event?"

"Me?" I asked, caught off guard.

"Yes. Why not? The food here is too pretentious." She wrinkled her nose and shook her head.

While I'd had the same thought myself, I wasn't sure how the club would feel about me stepping on their toes that way. "I don't know…"

"And of course, you'd supply the wine. Lord knows it would be fitting. Chas did enjoy that Petite Sirah of yours." Alison barked out a sardonic laugh again.

No way would I be serving my Petite Sirah at the memorial for the man who died drinking it. However, with all the cancellations, I could use the work. And the Links set were exactly the type of client I was trying to court. As morbid as a memorial was, any chance to get my food and wine in front of guests was a good one.

"If Vivienne would like me to cater the event, have her call me. I'd be happy to," I told Alison.

She nodded and gave me a satisfied smile as if that was settled, and went back to her glass.

I mumbled a farewell and made my escape. I had a feeling not many people said no to Alison Price, and I wasn't about to be the first.

* * *

By the time I got back to the lounge, Ava was saying her goodbyes to her father, and I filled her in on the fact that David had a prescription for the drugs that killed Chas and the exchange I'd witnessed between Vivienne and the *Godfather* reject as we waited for the valet to bring our cars around.

"Seems suspicious. This heated argument right after her husband dies," Ava said, nodding as if she liked this new angle.

"Agreed." Though I had no proof the exchange had anything to do with her husband's death.

"Any idea who this guy is?" Ava asked.

"I think Vivienne called him Trask." I paused. "But I have no idea if that's a first or last name."

"Okay. Stocky guy named Trask. That's a start."

I shot her a look. "Are you being sarcastic?"

"Who me? Never." She winked at me.

"Maybe Jenny knows who he is," I decided as my Jeep came up to the curb.

"Follow me home, and we'll find out," Ava offered, exchanging her own ticket for the keys to her GTO.

I did, my head churning with theories, ideas, and way too much imagination on the ride to Silver Girl.

We found Jenny upstairs in the loft, feet tucked up under her on the sofa, wearing an oversized T-shirt and sweats that looked like she'd slept in them. The red rimming her eyes hadn't improved much, and the perpetual sniffling of grief was still her constant companion. I felt for her. I remembered the days after my dad had passed away as a blur of tissues and tears too.

"Trask?" she repeated after I described the guy to her. Then she shook her head. "Doesn't sound familiar."

"Maybe he worked at Price Digital? Or was a friend of Chas's? Or Vivienne's?" I prompted. Though the exchange I'd witnessed had seemed far from friendly.

But Jenny shook her head. "Sorry. I don't think I ever met him."

"It was worth a shot," Ava said. She got up from the sofa and went into the kitchen. "Tea anyone?" she called.

"No thanks," Jenny mumbled. "I'm kind of tea'd out."

I watched Jenny as Ava brewed a cup of chamomile for herself. Jenny seemed so genuinely grief stricken. I phrased my next statement carefully.

"I met with Sadie Evans," I told her.

She sniffed, her eyes meeting mine. "He was sleeping with her, wasn't he?"

I nodded slowly. "Sorry."

She shrugged. "I had a feeling he was." She paused. "Look, I know my brother was no saint. But he was a good person. Deep down."

Way deep down, if what I was hearing from everyone else in his life was any indication. I hesitated to tell her that it was her brother who'd wanted her fired from Price Digital to keep his affair a secret.

"Sadie said she ended it with him before he died," I told her instead.

Jenny frowned. "That's odd."

My radar pricked up. "What's odd?"

"Well, just that she said she ended it. I…" She paused, looking sheepish for a moment. "I kind of overheard something.

I didn't want to say anything because I wasn't sure it meant anything."

"What did you overhear?" Ava asked, suddenly back in the living room, kettle abandoned now on the stove.

"Well, it was just a conversation between Chas and Sadie. Like I said, it didn't really mean anything to me at the time. Even if he had been sleeping with Sadie, which I wasn't sure of, well, I just took it as a lover's spat, you know? But I didn't know anything for sure, you know?"

No, I didn't know. She was talking in circles. "What did you hear, Jenny?"

She licked her lips, looking guilty again. "It was the day before Sadie fired me. Chas was in Sadie's office, and I was really just walking by. I was taking some paperwork to HR. But Sadie's door was open, and I heard them talking."

"What did you hear?" Ava asked for the third time.

More lip licking. "They were talking about a divorce."

That was the bombshell I was waiting for. "Divorce? You mean between Chas and Vivienne?"

She shrugged. "I kind of assumed so. Sadie was asking what was taking so long, and Chas said he needed time."

"How did Sadie respond to that?" I asked, envisioning the slinky power-hungry woman. If she'd been pressuring Chas to divorce Vivienne, it didn't sound like she'd tired of his company like she'd told me.

"Sadie wasn't happy," Jenny told us. "She accused him of stalling and said it wouldn't wait forever."

"It? What 'it'?"

"I don't know. She didn't say."

"And then?"

She shrugged. "Then Chas saw me, and I left and took the forms to HR." She paused again. "Sorry I didn't say anything before. I just…well, I figured if things were rocky between Chas and Vivienne, that was his business, you know? I don't even know if Vivienne knew he was contemplating divorce. And I still thought it was possible that Sadie was just a sympathetic ear in it all, you know?"

Jenny seemed to have a habit of seeing the best in people. It was a trait I didn't share at the moment, suddenly seeing motives for murder everywhere. If Chas had refused to divorce Vivienne, had Sadie gone woman scorned on him in a fit of anger? Or, had Vivienne gotten wind of Chas's plans and ended the marriage on her terms instead of in a messy public divorce?

Of course, I realized this new development didn't look all that great for Jenny either. Vivienne and Chas had had a prenup. If Chas left her for Sadie, he was likely to get very little—no more expensive gifts and no more funding for Jenny and her ailing parents either. And at the rate Chas purportedly burned through money, what little he had wouldn't have lasted long. But if Chas died first and Jenny was the sole heir of his estate… well, something was better than nothing.

I shook that thought out of my mind. This whole thing was making me way too suspicious. Of everyone. I much preferred Ava's optimistic outlook.

"That's a fabulous motive for murder!" Ava said, eyes shining.

So much for optimistic.

"What is?" Jenny asked, turning her attention to Ava.

"The other woman whose lover won't leave his wife."

"You're forgetting that Sadie wasn't at the Spanish party," I reminded her.

Ava waved that off. "She could have hired someone to do it. The woman's loaded."

I was about to point out that murderers for hire weren't exactly taking out billboard ads along the highway, when a knock sounded at the door. A loud one.

I could see Jenny almost physically jump at the sound.

My eyes cut to Ava. "Expecting someone?"

She shook her head and crossed to the front door, checking the peephole.

I could tell from her body language that it wasn't good, even before she uttered the words. "It's Detective Grant."

Jenny looked from Ava to me. "W-what does he want?"

I shrugged. "I don't know."

The knock sounded again, more insistent this time, and Ava pulled the door open, allowing the detective entry.

"Ms. Barnett. Ms. Oak," he said, nodding to each of us in turn.

I nodded back. "Detective Grant. Don't tell me you have a search warrant for Ava's stemware too?"

He shook his head, not even the slightest hint of humor on his face. "No, I'm here to talk to Miss Pacheco."

"Me?" Jenny tucked her feet in closer, almost as if shrinking into the sofa to avoid being seen.

He nodded.

"Has there been a new development?" I asked, fear collecting in my belly.

He pulled his attention away from Jenny to meet my eyes. The gold flecks in them were still today, almost as if whatever news he had was so sobering that even his eyes were dulled by it. "The CSI team has finished processing the contents of Mr. Pennington's car."

"The Lamborghini?" Ava asked.

He nodded again. "I'd like to ask Jenny a few questions about it."

"I-I don't know anything about Chas's car," Jenny said, her voice small.

"You rode to the winery in it the night of the party, correct?"

Jenny nodded. "Yes, I-I came in with Chas. He was held up at work, so he picked me up on the way. We were late."

"Did he drive you often, Ms. Pacheco?"

I narrowed my eyes, trying to figure what he was getting at.

"No, actually," Jenny answered. "I mean, I think I'd been in his car once or twice but not regularly."

"Once or twice. When would this have been?"

"What is this about?" I cut in, stopping Jenny from answering. It was clear Grant was trying to get her to say something, and whatever it was, I had a bad feeling Jenny might want a lawyer present.

Grant turned toward me, his expression unreadable. "We found alprazolam in Chas's car."

Ava scoffed. "Not surprising. Chas was into all sorts of drugs. Coke even!"

One of Grant's dark eyebrows arched her way.

"So I heard," Ava mumbled, shooting me a guilty look.

"Xanax is a common drug," I argued. "Tons of people have prescriptions for it. *Including* his stepson," I pointed out.

Grant paused. "David Allen?"

I nodded, feeling a lift of pride at supplying that tidbit of information. "Yes."

"How do you know that?" Grant asked, his face a granite slab of zero emotion.

"I know lots of things you don't know," I countered.

Grant narrowed his eyes at me. "*I* knew about David Allen's prescription. We've looked into everyone close to the victim with legal access to the drug. What I wanted to know was how *you* knew."

"Oh." I bit my lip feeling sheepish. Right. Of course Grant already knew. Not much got past him. "So what does this have to do with Jenny?" I asked, quickly deflecting.

Grant switched his focus, giving Jenny a hard look. "The pill found in her brother's car is the same concentration as Jenny's prescription."

My eyes shot to my friend who was still trying to be invisible on Ava's sofa. "*You* had a prescription for Xanax?" I blurted out before I could stop myself. Why had Jenny withheld that from us?

"I-I-I guess. I mean, yes, I take Xanax. For my anxiety. I-it's not something I like to talk about. It's embarrassing."

I closed my eyes and let out a long breath, wondering if Jenny had any idea how guilty she looked.

"And you knew this?" I asked Grant.

He nodded. "As I said, we looked into several people's prescriptions."

"Several?" I jumped on the word. "Who else?"

"I'm not at liberty to share that information."

I had a feeling it was his favorite phrase.

"Well, just because Jenny's Xanax was in Chas's car, that does not mean it was *her* Xanax that killed him," Ava reasoned.

Grant didn't say anything. And that fear in my belly grew into a gnawing ball.

"There's more, isn't there?" I almost hated to ask the question.

He turned those dark eyes my way again, this time a hint of sympathy in their depths. "Jenny's gotten prescriptions from four different doctors this year."

Jenny looked down at her feet. "So? I'm anxious a lot."

Grant ignored her, continuing. "I'm guessing the first doctor wouldn't refill your prescription so soon. That he suspected you were overusing the drugs."

"I wasn't!" Jenny protested. "Honestly!"

"You were giving them to Chas," I said, pieces falling into place.

Jenny was quiet, her eyes going from me to Grant. Finally she looked back down at the floor. "Yes," she said softly.

"Oh Jenny," I let out on a sigh.

"I'm sorry!" she said, tears on her cheeks again. "Look, I didn't mean to. At first I noticed some pills missing here and there, but I thought maybe I'd just forgotten about taking them. But then I found Chas going through my medicine cabinet one day when he was at my place, and he confessed that he'd taken them. He said he was just too anxious around Vivienne and her friends—that he didn't feel like he fit in. It wasn't his fault! He didn't want her to know, so…well, so I agreed to supply them for him."

Knowing he had a stash of cocaine in his office, Chas was more likely abusing the Xanax as a quick way to come down when he needed to. A dangerous practice.

"Wait—does this mean that Chas took the lethal dose of Xanax on his own?" Ava asked. I could see confusion etched on her face.

I looked to Grant, thinking that would be too easy. And wouldn't explain why he was here.

He shook his head. "No. The ME thinks he likely took a regular dose of the drugs that afternoon, before arriving at the party. Then, someone who knew he already had alprazolam in his system administered a further lethal dose later that evening."

"Which would explain such a high quantity," I mused out loud.

Grant nodded.

"Anyone could have known Chas was taking Xanax," Ava protested.

"But Jenny *did* know. And it was *her* fingerprints in his car and on the glass he was holding, which contained residue of the alprazolam. And she's the one who benefits from her brother's will. All of which leads us to just one place." He paused.

If I had to guess, it was not for dramatic effect as much as a reluctance to go forward. Reluctance that he apparently got over, as his voice forced out the words, "Jennifer Pacheco, you're under arrest for the murder of your brother, Chas Pennington."

CHAPTER FOURTEEN

"You have the right to remain silent. Anything you say can and will be used against you in a court of law. You have the right to an attorney. If you cannot afford one, one will be appointed by the court."

The words came out in a blur of Ava flapping her arms and shouting in protest, Jenny dissolving into sobs, and Grant's booming voice going on in a flat monotone as he recited the warnings we'd all heard a thousand times on cop shows. I might have found it amusing that it was happening in real life if it hadn't been so horrific that it was happening in *my* real life.

Sure, Jenny had made some bad decisions and left out some vital information. And had a serious blind spot where her brother's shortcomings were concerned. But that seemed to be an overarching theme with the women in his life. And I still didn't see her as a cold-blooded killer. Grant might have the murder weapon, but he hadn't seen Jenny's grief over the last few days. Anyone who had would realize how real it was and that there was no way Jenny could have hurt Chas.

"This is an outrage," Ava yelled as Grant gently eased Jenny off the sofa and led her by the elbow toward the front door. "This is nuts. Jenny didn't hurt anyone. This is…this is…wrongful arrest! This is going to cost the sheriff big bucks."

While I admired Ava's loyalty, I couldn't see wrongful arrest sticking. As far as I could see it, Grant had every right to arrest Jenny based on the evidence. The only problem was, Grant's current evidence was wrong. Or at least, it was pointing him in the wrong direction.

I promised Jenny I'd have my accountant, Shultz, track down an attorney for her and have someone meet her at the station to post bail. I wasn't sure she heard me through her sobbing, but I hoped it at least made her feel less alone. Where said bail would come from, I wasn't sure. I suddenly wondered how quickly one could unload a Lamborghini.

"Jenny didn't do this," I told Grant, trying one last time to appeal to his sense of decency. "I know it looks bad, but…but there were other shady characters in Chas's life."

He paused, giving me his attention now. "Shady?"

I nodded. "He-he was organizing illegal poker games," I said, glancing briefly at Ava, hoping I hadn't just tipped our hand.

But apparently Grant was one step ahead of us, as usual, as he just nodded. "I'm aware of his gambling habits."

Drat. Okay, I tried again. "Are you aware he was also having an affair with Sadie Evans and she wanted him to leave his wife?"

That one got him. Two dark eyebrows rose toward his hairline. "Really? And how do you know this?"

"Jenny told me," I said.

The eyebrows fell. "Jenny told you," he said flatly.

Okay, maybe his prime suspect wasn't the most credible source in his eyes.

"Well, well…what about Trask!" I didn't know why I blurted it out except pure desperation. I could feel Ava tense behind me. It was a huge shot in the dark, as we had no idea who he was to Vivienne or if he even knew Chas.

But apparently the name meant something to Grant, as his features went dark. "Joe Trask?"

Sure, Joe. Let's go with that. "Yes," I said defiantly, lifting my chin with false bravado.

"What does he have to do with this?"

"I saw him arguing with Vivienne Price-Pennington. *Threatening* her," I amended.

His eyes softened with something akin to genuine concern. "Stay away from Trask, Emmy," he told me.

I licked my lips, the sudden use of my first name unnerving. "Why?" I countered.

He shook his head. "He's not the type of guy you want to get involved with."

Nothing about this murder was anything I wanted to get involved with. But there I was—involved up to my neck.

I opened my mouth to ask just what type of guy this Trask was, but Grant ran right over me.

"I'll be in touch about Jenny's bail."

And with that, he was gone.

Ava slammed the door behind him with more force than was strictly necessary. "That smug, arrogant, ruthless, sonofa—"

"He was just doing his job," I stopped her.

Ava turned to me, her eyes wide, her mouth stuck in the open position. "Emmy Oak, don't tell me you've fallen for that bad boy charm and taken his side!"

"I haven't fallen for anything!" I protested. Maybe a bit too loudly. "And there are no sides." I shook my head, sinking into the sofa Jenny had just vacated, suddenly feeling as if my every limb was made of lead. "He's just following the evidence."

"But Jenny didn't do it!" Ava yelled.

"I know." I paused. "But it looks bad for her."

Ava plopped down beside me. "It really does, doesn't it?" She sighed. "So who do you think this Joe Trask guy is?"

I shook my head. "I don't know." I replayed the look in Grant's eyes, the genuine concern hidden behind his gold flecks as he'd warned me off the man. "But I think we should find out."

* * *

After calling Shultz, who promised to send a defense attorney to meet Jenny at the precinct, we spent the next hour with our good friend Google. And by late afternoon, we had the lowdown on one Joseph Trask. Or as he was known, Mr. Fast Money—at least according to his website.

The same bushy brows and oversize nose stared back at me from Ava's laptop screen, his stocky frame standing behind a glass case filled with gold and silver jewelry, gemstone-encrusted rings, and various antique weaponry. Fast Money was a pawn shop located in the East Bay, where Trask promised he'd turn over grandma's silver into cold, hard "fast" cash on the spot. According to the reviews online, it looked like Trask was a tough negotiator, earning several disgruntled one-stars from people who felt they'd been bilked once they went home and found the going rate for their treasures on eBay. I wondered if pawnbrokers cared much about online reviews.

However, the deeper we dug, the more it looked like the pawn shop was just one part of Mr. Fast Money's business…the legit part. According to a few insinuations on My Nosey Neighbor dot com, and a quick browse of the county court records, Trask's real business was not so much in trading your gold high school class ring for a Benjamin, but in loaning money with no questions asked, with a healthy interest rate attached, and a very strict payment-due policy. One that might include a couple of kneecaps as late fees.

"Grant was right," Ava decided as she finished reading a *Sonoma Index-Tribune* article out loud. "This guy is bad news."

I nodded. The column was all about how usury charges against Trask had been dropped when the witness with the wonky kneecaps had disappeared just before the trial. I shuddered, hoping he'd taken a long vacation to the Midwest and not to the bottom of the Bay.

"So what is a woman like Vivienne Price-Pennington doing mixed up with a loan shark?" I asked.

Ava shrugged. "Maybe her finances aren't as healthy as everyone has been led to believe?"

I nodded. "Possibly. But I can't imagine her being turned down for a loan from a regular bank. Or not being able to raise funds from investors or a VC firm, for that matter. Her name alone carries that much weight."

"True." Ava nodded. "Okay, well maybe it wasn't her debt they were discussing. Maybe David is the one Trask lent money to?"

I liked the sound of that. "David was gambling at each of Chas's games. Robby said he was a winner, but maybe he was mistaken. Or, maybe David lost more often than he won. Robby wasn't at every game," I told her. I'd checked. While she'd googled, I'd scrolled through all my photos of Chas's records to see how often the R.B. initials had shown up, and it had only been a scant few times—nothing in the last three weeks. I couldn't tell if he'd owed money to Chas at the time of his death, but the figures next to his name had been minimal compared to others. Like David's.

"So, David loses big at Chas's poker games," Ava said, thinking out loud. "He needs cash to cover his losses, so he turns to Joe Trask, Mr. Fast Money. Only, he can't pay Trask back, because he just keeps losing. So he offs Chas to erase the debt there, and has Mom try to work things out with Trask in an effort to keep his kneecaps intact." She paused, nodded. "I like it."

I had to admit, I did too. It was a solid theory. But at the moment that was all it was—theory. What we needed was proof. At least enough to refute Grant's proof that Jenny was his man. Or woman.

"I think we should visit Trask."

Ava turned to face me. "Did you not hear Grant?"

I shrugged. "Since when do I take orders from Detective Grant?"

A slow smile took over her features. "Good point. Okay, I'm right behind you, Lacey."

CHAPTER FIFTEEN

The Fast Money Pawnshop was located in a poorly maintained historic building in the city center of Vallejo. The awning was faded, the windows had bars on them, and a sign screamed in bright red neon that they were open 24 hours.

I beeped my Jeep locked twice, praying it still had all four tires when I came back, and Ava and I pushed through the front doors.

The interior pretty much matched the exterior—seedy, utilitarian, and giving an overall impression of needing some antiseptic and a facelift. Glass cases lined the back wall, filled with all manner of jewelry, collectibles, and antiques shoved together in a jumble that spoke of too much inventory and not enough organization. The walls were covered in framed paintings—everything from modern art to large gilded frames filled with oil paintings of hunting scenes. And a few guitars and guns took up space on the back wall. The overall vibe was claustrophobic and a little sad, knowing all these treasures had been given up in desperation.

A six-foot-six guy dressed all in black stood by the door, arms crossed over his chest, eyes hard and assessing. Clearly security. A younger guy with tattoos up his neck was helping a couple at the engagement ring case, and a girl with about fifteen piercings in her face approached us.

"You here to pawn, sell, or buy?" she asked in a valley girl accent that was totally incongruent with her look.

"Uh, actually we were hoping to talk to Joe Trask," I told her.

"You got an appointment?"

I shook my head in the negative.

"Can I tell him what this is about?" she asked.

I paused, realizing I hadn't come up with a good cover story for being here. I was pretty sure that telling him we'd like to interrogate him about his whereabouts when Chas Pennington was killed wasn't going to get us very far.

But Ava jumped right in. "We'd like to see him about some jewelry," she said. She held out her arm, which was adorned with half a dozen silver bracelets of her own making.

Pierced Girl nodded. "Okay, hold on a sec. I'll see if he's free."

She disappeared into a back office.

"Nice one," I told Ava.

She shrugged. "Hey, if the price is right, I'd sell a couple of these. No reason we can't solve a murder *and* make a couple bucks, right?" She winked at me.

We didn't have much more time to discuss what the right price was, as Joe Trask emerged from the back, waddling his stocky frame up to the counter. He was dressed in another cheap suit that hung a little too long in the cuffs and tugged a little too tight around the middle.

"I hear you got something to sell me?" he said, his eyebrows hunkered down over beady eyes in a permanent scowl.

Ava stepped forward. "Yes. I have a few silver bracelets. I might like to sell them if you can give me a good price."

Trask took a cursory look at the bangles on her arm, nodded, then pulled out a square board covered in black velvet and laid it out on the glass case. "Can I take a closer look?" he asked.

Ava looked wary but relented, taking the bracelets off and setting them side by side on the black cloth. Trask picked up each one in turn and held it up, checking the marks.

"Where did you get these?" he asked.

"A shop in Sonoma. Silver Girl," Ava said, shooting me another wink.

"Hmm." He made a noncommittal grunting sound in the back of his throat.

"They're one of a kind," she continued. "Genuine argentum silver. Handmade by the artist."

He shrugged. "Well, someone may have sold you that line, but these look mass produced."

Ava frowned. "The artist seemed very trustworthy to me."

"Most con artists are."

"Con artists!" Ava's voice rose, causing the guy with the neck tattoos and the engaged couple to turn our way.

I shot her an elbow to the ribs, and she shut her mouth with a click. But her arms stayed crossed over her chest, her nostrils flaring.

Trask seemed oblivious to her anger and put the last bracelet down. "Yeah, these are cheaply made, probably in China somewhere. I can give you fifteen bucks a piece, but that's being generous."

"Fifteen?" Ava spat out. "I'll have you know, these go for over $100 apiece. *Well* over."

"Hey, what can I say, girl? You overpaid."

"They are art," Ava ground out through gritted teeth.

He shook his head. "I'll probably just have to melt them down for the silver value."

"Like heck you will!"

Trask looked from Ava to me, his perma-scowl deepening.

"Uh, what my friend means," I said, quickly stepping in before Ava riled up the shark, "is that we're surprised at such a low offer. My friend Vivienne said you did a fair business here."

"Vivienne?" His eyes narrowed at the name,

"Yes. Vivienne Price-Pennington. She's the one who told me about your shop."

Trask's eyes homed in on mine. "What kind of game are you playing, kid?"

I swallowed. "Game? No game. We just want to make a little money on my friend's bracelet—"

"Baloney!" he yelled, piercing me with a look that froze the words on my tongue. "Vivienne Price-Pennington ain't no friend of mine, and I doubt she's a friend of yours." The way he gave my outfit an up and down on that last statement had me seriously planning a shopping day. Was I that obviously not the upper crust?

"So what's really going on here?" Trask demanded

Ava shot me a look of panic. I took a deep breath. "Okay, fine. We're not here to pawn the bracelets. You're right."

His face softened a scooch with satisfaction. Who didn't like to be right?

"So what are you here for?" he asked.

"Information." I licked my lips, feeling my mouth suddenly dry with nerves at confronting a guy with no regard for kneecaps. "Look, I know you argued with Vivienne over a debt." Which was half true. I knew they'd argued, but what it was over was pure guesswork.

Fortunately it seemed to be a good guess, as Trask nodded. "She tell you that?"

"Yes," I lied.

He nodded again. "Okay, fine. Let's hypothetically say that's true. What's it to you?"

"How much money are we talking?" Ava asked.

"Five hundred."

"Dollars?" Ava asked.

He shot her a look. "What do I look like, a piggy bank? G's, honey. Five hundred thousand."

Oh wow. That far exceeded anything in Chas's little black book. David must have been gambling elsewhere too. "So Vivienne agreed to pay off her son's debt?"

Trask's bushy brows drew down over his eyes like two unruly caterpillars. "Son?" He shook his head and barked out a laugh. "I guess the guy was young enough to be her kid, but ain't no mother ever married her son before that I know."

I blinked at him, the meaning sinking in. "Wait—it was *Chas Pennington* who owed you five hundred thousand dollars?"

Trask nodded, his gaze going from me to Ava. "Yeah. I guess your 'friend' Vivvy didn't tell you that?"

I ignored the question, my brain trying to play catch up. If Chas had been running the poker games, he should have been raking in the cash. Sure, he had a spending habit, but I couldn't see him going through all the amounts listed in his book as well as needing a loan that size. At least, not desperately enough to resort to taking it from Trask.

That is, unless those numbers we saw weren't winnings but *losses*. Could it be that the initials next to the dollar amounts were people Chas had owed money *to* and not people he'd profited *from*?

"When did Chas borrow this money?" I asked.

Trask shrugged. "A little here, a little there. Kid liked to play poker."

"So we've heard," Ava mumbled.

He turned his attention to her. "Yeah well, lucky me, he was terrible at it. Kept losing. Said he didn't want his old lady to find out he'd been gambling with her cash, so he needed a loan. You know, just till he could win some back." Trask laughed, showing off a gold incisor, clearly enjoying the humor in anyone thinking they could win back gambling losses.

"And now that he's dead, you're after Vivienne to pay his debt," I surmised.

Trask shrugged. "Hey, a debt's a debt." He paused, looking from Ava to me, his eyes narrowing again. "Look, you're not here trying to say I had anything to do with Chas's death?"

I held my hands up in a surrender motion. "Did I say that?" Trust me, I did *not*. I was not in the habit of calling big guys with gold teeth and criminal records murderers. Even if the cement shoes fit.

"Look, I had no reason to want Chas Pennington dead." Trask spread two hairy hands out wide. "Why would I? The guy was my best customer. Besides, I knew his old lady was good for it."

I had to admit he had a point. Why kill the goose that was laying golden gambling chips on a regular basis? However, Vivienne Price-Pennington suddenly had a big reason to want her husband dead—a five hundred thousand dollar one. Had she killed him to stop the hemorrhage of money? Out of anger that he'd been gambling behind her back, losing at his own games no less?

"Just curious, what kind of interest did you charge Chas on that loan?" Ava asked

That gold tooth flashed again as Trask did a big grin. "Honey, you don't wanna know."

He was right. We probably didn't. The less I knew about loan sharking, the better for my status as an accessory after the fact.

"Hey, Vivienne should be glad to keep it all in the family, you know?"

I paused. "What do you mean by that?"

Trask barked out a laugh. "I mean the guy Chas paid the most green to was his stepson."

"David Allen?" I blurted out before I could stop myself.

Trask nodded. "Sure. The kid had a knack for winning, from what I hear. He was taking Chas to the cleaners. Or, to here, I guess." He spread his arms wide again, the humor in his face disconcerting considering we were talking about a dead man.

"Chas was borrowing money from *you* to pay back *David Allen*?" I clarified.

"And others. Chas lost a lot. But, yeah, the bulk of it went to the stepson. So, like I said, Viv ain't got all that much to complain about."

"Just the interest," Ava mumbled.

Trask shot her a look. "Legal max. That's all I charge. Anyone tells you different, they gonna be sorry."

While I knew he was lying about the first part of that statement, I had a feeling he was being dead honest about the second.

We thanked him for his time and bugged out of there quickly, before we could inadvertently make ourselves sorry for anything.

"So do we believe him?" Ava asked as we pulled onto the freeway.

"I don't see that he has a reason to lie," I responded. "I mean, about Chas's debt at least."

"So it's not the sleazy neighborhood loan shark who killed Chas?" Ava sounded disappointed.

I shrugged. "I can't think of a reason he would. He's right—keeping Chas alive seems like it was in his best interest."

"Well, I guess the same could be said for David Allen now, too," she mused. "I mean, if Chas was consistently losing money to David, why would David kill his cash cow?"

"Unless Chas got tired of paying David and decided to tell Vivienne about it," I offered.

"But wouldn't Chas have to confess he'd been gambling too?"

I nodded. "True. But who do you think Viv would be more quick to forgive—her hot young husband or her leech of a son?"

"Good point," Ava agreed. "She did seem to have a bit of a blind spot where Chas's faults are concerned."

"Either that," I said, playing devil's advocate, "or she finally opened her eyes and had enough of Chas making a fool of her and killed him."

Ava shook her head. "All these people who had reason to want Chas dead. And to think Grant has locked up the one person in Chas's life who actually *liked* him."

I would have laughed at the irony if the thought didn't make me picture Jenny in a cold, dark cell alone. I wondered how long she'd have to be there before she got a bail hearing. I prayed Shultz's lawyer was working hard to get her out. And that she could afford to pay his fees when she did.

I dropped Ava off at her loft and drove on autopilot back to the winery, my mind churning over each of our suspects and just how, exactly, each could have done Chas in. They all had ample reasons, all had opportunity—except maybe Sadie, but there was nothing saying she didn't find someone else to administer the lethal dose. In fact, for all we knew, she could have given it to Chas himself, telling him it was any manner of recreational drugs that it appeared Chas was interested in. Chas might not have known the difference. White powder all looked pretty much the same. Especially when you were already drunk off amazing Petite Sirah.

The sun was sinking down behind the hills as I made my way up the gravel drive, creating a watercolor masterpiece of pinks, purples, and pale oranges across the horizon. It was like a postcard, beckoning travelers to the relaxation that awaited them in wine country, and thoughts of murder, gambling, and drugs seemed a million miles away from the serene scene. I only wished they were.

Mine was the sole car as I pulled into the lot, save the staffs'. Another slow day at Oak Valley.

I locked my Wrangler and made my way into the main kitchen. While I'd shopped for a meal earlier, I suddenly felt the day had drained me, and I was infinitely glad to see Conchita had been there on her day off after all, leaving behind a Mexican Lasagna that had a Post-it with reheating instructions. I smiled to myself. I might be a trained chef, but Conchita was still the queen of her kitchen and left me instructions on how to reheat.

I did, enjoying the ooey gooey cheesy goodness with a glass of Zinfandel on the back patio as I watched the rest of the sun dissolve into the hills, the sky going a warm blue until the first stars started to twinkle above and the air chilled.

I quickly cleaned up and made the rounds, making sure the kitchen, tasting room, and offices were all locked up for the night. I was just closing up the doors to the cellar when, on a whim, instead of locking them, I stepped inside. It was cold and dark, just the way the wines liked it. I tugged my light sweater tighter around myself as I stepped inside and turned on the light switch. I hadn't been down there since I'd found Chas. For one, the police had had the cave well cordoned off for days to process it for evidence. And after it had been released, well, it just hadn't seemed like my favorite place in the world.

I took a tentative step inside.

Predictably, there were few remnants of the tragedy that had taken place there. The glass had been cleaned up, save for a few sparkling shards lurking in the corners as the light caught them. The body was long gone, and the spilled wine had been cleaned up as well, leaving only the slightest stain on the old tiles, indistinguishable from the countless others to anyone who hadn't witnessed the murder scene firsthand.

If I'd hoped for some clue or inspiration about who the killer had been, I was sorely disappointed. Which, as I turned to go again, wasn't surprising, as according to Grant, the killer had likely never been in the cellar to begin with, administering the lethal drugs sometime during the party. While this dark, cold, isolated setting seemed more fitting for a murder, the reality was a party guest had nonchalantly slipped poison into a glass of wine in plain sight during a lively gathering. The thought had me tugging my sweater closer again, a chill hitting my bones.

I turned out the lights and locked the door, walking the path from the cave toward my cottage.

But I only got a few steps when I heard a sound.

I instantly froze, listening in the dark.

Nothing.

I was probably letting my imagination get the better of me. No one was here. It must have been a bird or opossum or some other nocturnal creature. I was alone at the winery.

I shook off the fight-or-flight response surging through me, instead trying to focus on the hot bath, soft bed, and mind-numbing TV awaiting me at my cottage.

Only I never got to it.

Two steps from my front door, I heard the sound again—this time right behind me. I instinctively turned to see what or who was making it.

But instead all I saw was black, as pain exploded at my temple and the ground surged up to meet me.

CHAPTER SIXTEEN

I was standing at the top of the hill with my father. Only he wasn't sick and pale, like I'd last seen him, but standing tall and strong, surveying the vines with a small smile of satisfaction on his lips that said he was in his element. I opened my mouth to speak—to tell him just how much I'd missed this. Only no sound came out. All I could hear was the wind picking up behind the trees, rustling the leaves. I tried to call out to my dad, yell, scream, alert him to my presence, but he seemed in his own world, completely focused on the landscape, expressions serene and happy. I tried to yell again.

"Dad, it's me. Emmy! Emmy!"

But he didn't hear me. In fact the words didn't even sound like my voice. They felt disconnected, far away.

"Emmy! Emmy?"

They grew louder, and my dad, the vines, and the rustling leaves began to fade away, replaced with darkness. And pain. A searing, throbbing pain at my temple as I struggled to open my eyes.

"Emmy?"

I blinked, realizing the voice was not entirely in my dream. Detective Christopher Grant bent over me, the fleck in his hazel eyes dancing in a frenzy as his dark eyebrows drew over them in concern. "Emmy? Emmy, can you hear me?" he asked.

I blinked again, the movement taking great effort. "Yes," I croaked out and nodded. Ouch. Bad idea. The pain spread around my head like a wildfire.

"Don't move," Grant instructed. "I'll call an ambulance."

"No," I said, finding my voice. "No, I'm fine." Or I was pretty sure I would be. After a bottle of aspirin. I pushed myself into a semi-sitting position on the cold pavers of the pathway and took stock of my body. I wiggled toes, fingers, legs. Everything seemed to be in working order, even if my head did feel a little fuzzy, almost like it wasn't quite connected to my body. I spied a large rock lying on the stones near me and cringed as I noticed a drop of blood on it. I gingerly reached a finger up to my head, feeling a trickle of wet sticky substance, confirming the blood was mine.

"You're bleeding." Grant realized it too. "I'm calling an ambulance, and I'm not taking no for an answer." He pulled out his cell.

"Well *no* is the answer," I said. I covered his hand with one of my own, preventing him from dialing. "I don't have insurance," I admitted. What could I say? Mom's medical bills were high enough that there was little left over to cover the exorbitant cost of medical insurance in California. I figured I was young and healthy enough to wing it for a year. At least until the winery was in the black. "I'm fine," I said again, hoping that statement sounded more confident than I felt.

Grant paused, his eyes going to my hand covering his.

I awkwardly pulled it back.

"Let me help you inside," he offered, supporting me as I slowly got to my feet.

I'm proud to say I only swayed a little. I gave my keys to Grant, not trusting my hands to be steady enough to open the door. At least not while trying to maintain the appearance of being "fine."

"What happened?" he asked as he gingerly guided me to the sofa.

I sank down, never more grateful I'd opted for squishy, soft furniture rather than uncomfortably fashionable. "I-I don't know," I told him honestly.

Grant sat beside me, concern still etched on his face as he gave me an assessing once-over. "You've got a nasty bump on your head." His fingers went up to my temple, gently brushing my hair behind my ear to inspect it.

I shivered, more from the intimate gesture than the sting of pain there.

"I think someone hit me," I confessed.

"Who?" The word had a sharp edge to it. Almost a dare.

I shrugged. "I don't know. I didn't see anyone. But I heard a noise."

"What sort of noise?"

I bit my lip. "I don't know." Some great witness I was. "I-I thought I heard something near the cave when I was locking up."

"The cave?"

"The wine cellar," I explained. "Then I heard it again as I was approaching my cottage. But I blacked out before I could see what. Or who."

"Oh, Emmy." It came out on a sigh, as if exasperation was mixed with relief that a bump on the head was all I'd gotten. The hard angles of his face relaxed a little, giving him a hint of vulnerability that was way too tantalizing. His hand went to my head again, lingering just a little longer than was strictly necessary to inspect my wound.

For a moment it felt like we were just two humans, and not a cop and a struggling business owner keeping secrets and sneaking into places she shouldn't. Though, in my defense, the sneak that evening had been breaking into *my* winery.

"I think you should check out where David Allen was tonight," I said.

And just like that, the moment was over. Grant pulled his hand back, leaning into the sofa. "David Allen? You think he hit you?"

I moved to nod but thought better of it. "Possibly. He had motive to want Chas dead."

The hazel flecks stopped dancing in Grant's eyes, their depths going darker. "A lot of people had motive to want Pennington dead."

"But I could see David doing it." Which was the truth. Both the murder and my head bashing. David seemed to fit the lurking-in-the-dark profile to a tee.

"That's hardly evidence. Unless you *did* see him."

"I told you, I didn't see anything. But I did find out that Chas owed David Allen a lot of money."

Grant frowned at me. "He owed a lot of people money."

"But what if Chas threatened to tell Vivienne that David was shaking him down? David could have lost his cushy lifestyle. And according to Trask, Chas owed David Allen half a million. That's plenty to kill over."

"Trask? Joe Trask?" Grant's jaw clenched, his eyes flashing.

Oops. Had I let that slip out? "Um, yes?" It came out more as a question.

"When did you talk to Joe Trask?" he demanded.

"Uh…I went to his shop earlier today?"

"In person?!"

"Umm…"

Grant let out a string of curse words that would have made my grandmother blush. "Emmy, this is not a game! You don't mess with people like Joe Trask. You could have been killed."

I raised an eyebrow at him. "Wait, are you saying that being hit on the head is *my* fault?"

He sighed and ran a hand through his hair. "What I'm saying is curiosity killed the cat."

I rolled my eyes. "Oh please. You're better than clichés, Grant."

He grinned, breaking through the tension. "Okay, how about this: there's a murderer on the loose, and you seem to be in their sights. Why, I'm not sure."

I had a guess. I was getting too close, asking too many questions. As cliché as it was, he was right—I was digging into something that someone wanted to keep under wraps. And unlike my feline counterparts, I only had one life. And I wanted to keep it, thank you very much.

"I'll be careful," I promised, meaning it.

"Thank you," he said, his voice missing that dangerous edge it usually held.

It was enough to melt a weaker woman at the knees.

"But don't you think that the fact someone hit me means I might be onto something?" I watched his reaction. His jaw squared again, the tension back. I tamped down a twinge of disappointment.

"Emmy…"

"No, listen. If Jenny killed her brother, why would anyone attack me? She's in jail."

"She made bail a couple of hours ago. She's staying with her parents, who just got into town. That's what I came to tell you."

"Oh." While I was glad she was home safe and sound, the timing wasn't ideal. "You could have told me that over the phone," I said.

He shrugged. "Where would the fun be in that?"

I paused. Was he flirting with me? I shook that thought out of my fuzzy head. My mind was playing tricks on me. Concussions did that.

"Okay, well, what reason would she have to attack me?" I countered.

"What makes you think these two events are connected?" he asked, his eyes intent on me.

I willed myself not to crack under his stare. "You think it's just coincidence?"

He sighed and shook his head. "No. I don't. But just because you poked your nose into someone's business that they'd rather keep private, that doesn't mean they killed Chas. It just means they don't much like you."

"Ouch." But he was right. I had no proof the two were connected. What I did have was a pounding headache, a dry mouth, and a sudden exhaustion that I could feel all the way to the tips of my toes.

It must have shown on my face, as the concern tugged at his eyebrows again. "You're going to have a hell of a bruise in the morning," he said softly. "I don't think you should be alone tonight."

Oh boy. I licked my dry lips, cursing my traitorous body for heating up in places that would also make my grandmother blush. "You don't?" I breathed out.

He shook his head slowly. "Do you have someone you can call?"

I cleared my throat. "Uh, yeah. Sure. I-I can call Ava."

He nodded. "I think that's best."

I tore myself away from his dancing eyes, giving my traitorous body a *down, girl* as I pulled out my cell and dialed Ava's number. I gave her the CliffsNotes version of the evening, and she promised she'd be there in ten minutes.

Nine minutes later she arrived in a flurry of ohmigod's and are-you-okay's. I gave her the detailed version of events, all the while watching Grant's concern fade back into his stoic cop demeanor. By the time I was finished and he was satisfied I wasn't in dire need of medical attention, he gave us both a curt nod goodbye and said he'd call in the morning.

As soon as he left, that exhaustion that had been dogging me all evening won over, and I collapsed into bed.

* * *

I awoke feeling like I'd been hit by a truck. Or maybe just a large rock. Either way, my head pounded, my mouth felt like a desert, and as I looked in the mirror, a purple bump sat on my temple and a large dark circle had blossomed around my right eye where I'd hit the ground. I gingerly blinked, wondering if I had enough concealer to cover it. After a shower, a blow dry, and a couple pounds of makeup, I decided I didn't. I opted for a pair of very large, very dark sunglasses instead, the lenses black and round, like Mickey Mouse's ears, which covered my black eye even if they did feel a tad dramatic.

I threw on a pair of skinny jeans, a dark shirt, and a warm caramel sweater that complemented my knee-high suede boots, and made my way to the living room, where the remnants of our impromptu sleepover lay in a rumpled heap on my couch. A Post-it told me Ava had gone to the main kitchen in search of coffee. I thought that was a fabulous idea.

I followed the heavenly smell of brewing French roast and cinnamon rolls toward the kitchen, and found Ava and Conchita deep in conversation, Ava regaling her with the tale of the attack the night before. Adding in just a few of her own embellishments. I could only imagine how the story would grow once Jean Luc added his dramatic flair to it. By noon I feared I'd be fighting off three ninjas and have a full body cast.

"Ay, Emmy," Conchita said when she spied me, enveloping me in a big hug.

"I'm fine," I told her. Though it came out more like "I've fibe," with my face mushed against her shoulder.

"*Ay, mija*!" she said, reverting to Spanish in the emotion of the moment as she lifted my sunglasses.

"It will heal," I told her.

She tsked her tongue, letting out a few more phrases in her native language as she fluttered over me and fussed, assessing every inch of me herself.

"I'm fine, really," I told her, sounding much more confident than my pounding head felt.

"Bacon," Conchita decided. "You need bacon."

Despite the pain, I felt a smile tug at the corners of my mouth. "You know me so well." And she was right. Bacon certainly wouldn't make the situation worse.

As she moved to the stove, I filled in the blanks Ava hadn't given her and set the record straight on a few of the exaggerations, finishing with my visit from Grant and his admission that, in this crime at least, Jenny seemed the innocent party.

"I don't buy it for a second that this isn't connected to Chas's murder," Ava said hotly.

I nodded. "I agree. Nothing was taken, nothing else disturbed. I think this was a warning."

Conchita gasped and made the sign of the cross.

"A warning I'll heed," I assured her.

Ava shot me a look. "Are you saying you're dropping the whole thing? Emmy Oak, that's not like you."

I shook my head, only mildly regretting it as a dull ache wrapped around my brain. "No, I'm saying I plan to be more careful. No more being alone outside after dark."

"I bet it was Trask," Ava said, shoving a bite of sugary glazed cinnamon roll into her mouth.

"I think that was Grant's fear too," I said.

"But why would he want that Chas dead?" Conchita asked. "I thought you said he was making a lot of money from him."

Ava shook her head. "I've been thinking about that. And, yes, he could have made a lot of money off him, *if* Chas had been paying him back. Which, he'd yet to do. Maybe Chas refused. Maybe Trask decided he'd have a better shot at convincing Vivienne to pay."

"But he didn't need to kill Chas for that," I pointed out. "He could have approached Vivienne anytime."

Ava chewed thoughtfully. "Okay, so what if Chas had something on Trask."

That was a new angle. "I'm listening," I told her.

"Well, maybe Chas told Trask he wasn't going to pay and threatened to go to the police if Trask didn't forgive the debt. Trask has been brought up on usury charges before."

"What is usury?" Conchita asked, scrunching up her nose.

"Loan sharking," I supplied, liking this new theory. "Your average desperate gambler might not have enough clout to get the authorities' attention. But if Chas Pennington somehow came to them with evidence of Trask's business, they might take note."

Ava nodded. "So, Trask offs Chas and tells Viv she has to cover the debt. It's a win-win for him."

"Just one problem," Conchita cut in.

We both turned to her.

"This loan shark wasn't at the Spanish party."

My hopes fell. "That's right."

"So maybe Trask didn't give Chas the drugs himself," Ava said, undeterred. "But he could have paid someone to do it. Maybe even one of the other guests? Who knows, maybe one of them owed Trask money, and this was his way of forgiving their debt?"

It was all very possible. And I could well see the seedy Trask braining me on the head without his lazy conscience blinking an eye. The thought of him slinking around the winery in the dark made me shiver, even in the cozy warmth of the kitchen, surrounded by scents of cinnamon, lattes, and bacon.

"I'd like to talk to Vivienne again," I decided.

Ava paused midbite. "Why?"

"I'd like to know just how much of Chas's extracurricular activities she knew about before he died." I sipped my coffee. "I feel like it's the key to everyone's motive."

"You think she'll see us again?"

I nodded. "I do. Because yesterday her mother asked me to cater the memorial." I paused to sip again as I thought through the plan. "We could say we need to go over the menu." Which, if I really was going to cater the event, was not a lie. Of course, I'd yet to be formally hired, but I could kill two birds with one stone.

Ouch. Poor choice of words. My hand went to my aching temple. I did not want to be the bird getting hit with the stone ever again.

CHAPTER SEVENTEEN

After breakfast, I called Vivienne. She confirmed that, yes, her mother had mentioned the catering job, yes, she did want us to work the event, and, yes, she was free to see us that morning.

When we arrived at the Price-Pennington estate, the Lurch look-alike butler let us in again, his lurking presence feeling even more resentful of visitors than on our last occasion as he led us to the lounge to await our hostess. Vivienne came in a moment later, again dressed in unrelieved black—this time in a pair of black cigarette pants, high-heeled ankle boots, and a blouse that billowed fashionably around her hips. Her makeup was subdued, though the diamonds at her ears and on her fingers seemed to shine even more brightly, as if in defiance to the somber mood.

"Thank you for coming," she told us, crossing to the bar on the far wall. "Drink?" she asked, pouring amber liquid into a glass.

I shook my head. It was just past ten.

"No thank you," Ava answered politely.

Vivienne shrugged and sipped from the glass. "Suit yourself." She paused, giving me a good look. "Those are *some* glasses. Late night?"

Instinctively, my hands went to the large frames covering the even larger bruise. "Something like that," I mumbled.

"Anyway, the memorial," she said, all business now. "It's going to be a small, intimate affair. I don't want the masses. No reporters, no media. Just close personal friends." She paused. "No more than a hundred people."

Ava and I were having a hard time finding *one* friend of Chas's, let alone a hundred. I had a feeling Vivienne had a blind spot where others' feelings about her husband were concerned too.

"You can do that on short notice?" Vivienne asked.

I nodded. "No problem."

"Good. I'm thinking just small bites, trays of things. Nothing fussy. Nothing too heavy."

"I can do some small plates and wine pairings. Maybe some beef filet crostini that would go well with our Pinot Noir. Possibly something with truffle to go with the Chardonnay?"

Vivienne nodded and waved her glass in my direction. "Sure. Fine. Whatever you think is best," she said, clearly not interested in the culinary details.

"Did you have a budget in mind for the catering?" Ava asked, giving me a sideways glance that said she was fishing for more than just the budget.

But Vivienne just fluttered a hand our way again as she took another sip. "Whatever you think is best."

"Really?" Ava pressed. "You're not concerned with costs? I mean, I would think that Chas's passing has been a bit of a financial burden."

Vivienne paused, her glass midway to her mouth. "Excuse me?"

Uh-oh. Had we pushed too far?

"Uh, you know, funeral costs, flowers, lawyers and such…" I trailed off, trying to cover. The last thing I wanted to do was get on Vivienne Price-Pennington's bad side. At best, she could ruin my reputation among the wine loving elite in town with a single word. At worst, she could be a cold-blooded killer, and it was never a good idea to upset one of those.

But she didn't seem to be buying it. She looked from Ava to me. "I don't think your friend *did* mean that, did you?" She cocked her head at Ava. Her eyes were calculating and cold, and I caught a glimpse of the woman who had ruined more than one life in the boardroom peeking through the grief stricken cougar facade.

Ava blinked, turning to me for help. "Uh, well…"

I decided the direct approach was best and stepped in. "I saw you talking to Joe Trask at the Links yesterday," I blurted out.

Vivienne swung her hard stare my way. For a moment I thought she was going to deny it—her jaw clenched, eyes narrowed. But finally she sighed audibly, her features going slack. "Yes. I agreed to meet Mr. Trask there."

"To talk about Chas's loan?" I prodded.

Her nostrils flared with emotion, but she nodded. "If you can call it that. With the interest he's charging, I'd call it highway robbery."

"Usury," Ava provided. "And it's illegal you know."

"I know," Vivienne snapped at her. "But how would that look to the board, huh? My husband using company funds for illegal gambling and then owing money to a loan shark?"

"Wait—*company* funds?" I thought of all the expense reimbursement requests we'd seen in Chas's office. Could it be the receipts had been faked in order to get company funds for his poker habits?

Vivienne sighed again. "Yes. Chas was skimming from Price Digital. It's my fault really." She waved her hand in the air as if waving aside any blame we might lay at Chas's dead feet. "He kept asking me for more money, increases to his allowance. At one point I just said no. I mean, it was getting extravagant. I asked what he needed the money for, but he just said he was helping out his family. Which, of course, I endorsed, but, really, how much did they need?"

Honestly? A lot more than Chas was *not* giving them, if Jenny's stories of her sick father were any indication. But I kept that opinion to myself as Vivienne continued.

"Anyway, I just finally told him no." She shook her head, her eyes filling with tears as she stared at a point across the room, reliving the scene in her mind. "I should have just let him have free rein with accounts. I mean, we *were* married."

"Did you know Chas was stealing from Price Digital before he died?" I asked, knowing I had to tread carefully here.

Vivienne let out another deep sigh and looked from Ava to me. "This doesn't leave this room."

We both nodded in agreement.

"I suspected. One of the managers in accounting told me Chas had been submitting a large number of requests lately. She'd even turned some down, but she thought I should know." Vivienne paused, sipping her drink. "So, I looked into it. And she was right. Chas was playing loose with the requests. He was submitting receipts for things I'd bought him, and claiming he needed reimbursement for them." She shook her head. "He doctored some receipts, inflating amounts. Some looked fabricated altogether."

"Did you confront him?"

She shook her head. "No." She paused, licking the mauve lipstick off her lips. "I covered for him." She choked back a guilty sob.

"You covered it up?" Ava asked.

She nodded, holding a tissue to her nose. "Look, I know it wasn't that Chas was bad. He was just weak. Easily tempted. And it was my fault. All of it. If I'd just given him the money he needed, he wouldn't have had to skim anything. So, I covered up the discrepancies."

"Even though he was continuing to gamble?"

She shook her head sadly. "I didn't know what the money was for at the time. I-I just suspected he liked nice things. Honestly, I didn't know!"

But she did know her husband was stealing from her. From the company she'd built from nothing, poured so much of her heart and soul into that she'd neglected her son most of his young life. I wondered…had it mattered what Chas wanted the money for? Or just that he was slimy enough to steal from the hand that fed him?

"You said that someone in accounting alerted you to Chas's receipts," Ava said. "What about Sadie? Did she know?"

At the mention of Sadie's name, the expression on Vivienne's face changed. Gone was the look of nostalgia and regret, replaced by that predatory boardroom shark coldness in her eyes again. "Why would Sadie know anything about it?"

Ava shrugged. "She *is* your partner."

"Yes, but it's *my* name on the door," Vivienne said defiantly. She shook her head. "I told you, Sadie didn't like Chas.

She said he was dead weight at the company. I don't think she had much to do with him at all."

Except have a secret affair with him. Either Vivienne was truly in the dark about her partner and her husband, or she was a top-notch actress.

Vivienne might not have known Chas was stealing money for gambling, but Sadie *had* known about the poker games. If she'd found out he was stealing from the company she'd just become a partner in, I wondered how Sadie would take that news.

Maybe Sadie Evans hadn't cared about Chas romantically after all. Maybe this wasn't so much a case of a woman scorned but a woman getting even with a thief.

* * *

Vivienne promised to have her assistant get back to me with the details of the memorial, and Ava and I left her pouring a second glass of whiskey. We found our way out of the house without the help of Lurch and jumped back into my Jeep.

"What do we think of Vivienne's cover-up?" Ava asked.

I shrugged. "We only have her word for it that she did cover it up."

"And didn't confront Chas in a deadly showdown?" Ava finished for me as I wound through the tree-lined streets back toward Oak Valley.

"Or that Sadie Evans didn't find out."

Ava nodded. "I noticed you asking about her. You think maybe Sadie found out and killed Chas before he could steal more of the company funds?"

"It's possible," I decided.

"I wonder if Jenny knew what he was up to," Ava said, looking out the window.

I spun on her. "What do you mean?"

"Well, just that Jenny covered up his Xanax use. And she did work at Price Digital. Maybe she covered for her brother there, too."

I bit my lip. That was something I didn't want to think about. It could only serve to paint Jenny in a more guilty light.

I was about to voice as much when a text popped in on my phone. I glanced away from the road just long enough to see Detective Grant's name on the display.

"Who is it?" Ava asked.

"Grant."

"Detective Hottie?"

I shot her a look. "He is not hot."

"Liar."

I grinned. "Okay, he's a little hot." I handed her the phone, turning my eyes back to the road. "Read it for me."

She swiped the text screen open. "*Just checking in. How are you feeling?*" she read out. Then added, "Aw, the big, bad detective cares."

I shot her a look. "He's just being thorough," I told her.

She shrugged. "He did seem pretty concerned about you last night."

"He's a cop. He has to be concerned." But I could feel my cheeks heating.

"You're blushing," Ava said, a big grin on her face. "Don't tell me you have a thing for Detective Hottie."

"No," I said defiantly. "No thing." My body might have had a minor attraction, but it definitely was not a *thing*.

I pulled up to the winery and parked next to Ava's GTO, and noticed another car in the lot—a shiny silver Mercedes with vanity plates that read MNYMAN1. I stifled an internal groan, fearing that I knew exactly who the "money man" in question was.

Sure enough, as soon as I said my goodbyes to Ava and made my way into the main building, Jean Luc approached, arms flapping in a tizzy.

"Zee banker man is in zee office, Emmy," he told me, wrinkling up his nose like he'd smelled overripe brie. "And he does not zeem very happy, *mon ami*."

Fabulous.

I thanked Jean Luc, took a deep breath, and steeled myself for the worst as I walked into my office to find Gene Shultz sitting in my desk chair, casually browsing the spreadsheets that were up on my computer screen as he waited for me. At my appearance, he looked up, a smile taking over his features.

"Emmy!" He shot to his feet, not even looking slightly guilty at having been caught peeking at my financials. His dark hair was going more salt than pepper, but his face was line-free—I suspected with some help of an excellent esthetician in The City—and his hands as he shook mine were excellently manicured. I suddenly felt butch next to him.

"Schultz. Always a pleasure," I fibbed.

"You're a terrible liar, Emmy."

"So I've been told," I mumbled. "Several times."

He grinned at me, showing off freshly whitened teeth that blinded me with their glare. "But, I'm a necessary evil in your life if you want to get this place operating in the black."

"Oh, I wouldn't go so far as to call you evil." I grinned back.

"Well, reserve that judgment until you hear what I have to say."

Uh-oh. I set my purse down on the desk with a thud and sank into the chair opposite my desk—usually reserved for visitors. I was keenly aware of the subtle power shift that Schultz had pulled off by planting himself in the chair behind the desk.

"Rip the Band-Aid," I told him. "What is it this time?"

Before he answered, he paused, studying me. "What's with the glasses?"

"Long story. Let's just say they're a fashion statement."

Gene raised one eyebrow. "Okay, let's say that."

"What did you need, Gene?" I asked, trying not to be short with him. It wasn't his fault I owed money, and the cancellations were pouring in, and I was about to go belly-up.

Gene dug his hand into the briefcase at his side, coming out with a newspaper, which he tossed on my desk.

I leaned forward to read it.

SONOMA'S DEADLY WINERY was the headline that jumped out at me.

I closed my eyes. I counted to ten. I took deep breaths. I opened them and still felt just as furious. So much for Zen.

"As you can imagine, this does not make my investors very happy," Schultz said.

"It doesn't make anyone very happy," I mumbled again.

"And," he went on, "unhappy investors pull the money to go somewhere safer. CDs. Bonds. Not financial institutions that back deadly wineries."

"We're not deadly!" I protested.

Schultz tapped the paper. "But everyone *thinks* you are. And what they think is what matters."

"No one reads actual papers anymore," I protested.

Schultz cocked his head to the side. "Nice try. It's online too."

"They arrested Jenny Pacheco," I told him, unsure if that helped my case or not.

Schultz shrugged. "That's lovely, but it's not filling seats in the bar, is it?" he asked, gesturing toward our empty tasting room.

I shook my head. "I will. I've got a big party coming up. Lots of influential people there." I did not elaborate that it was the memorial for the victim of the "deadly winery."

Schultz nodded. "Good, good. That's a start. But things need to turn around, Emmy. Quickly. It's one thing for me to keep the wolves at bay and extend your payment deadlines. It's quite another for me to convince said wolves to extend any more credit when they're reading headlines like these." He wagged a manicured finger at me.

I bit the inside of my lip. Credit was something we sorely needed when the harvest came.

"Right, understood. Turn the tide of public opinion. On it," I promised.

Schultz flashed me his megawatt smile again. "That's my girl. Now, hop to it. And no more of this drama stuff, yeah?" he said, gesturing to the paper.

I nodded. "Got it." As if the drama was my fault. Trust me—a drama-free life was totally on my agenda.

Schultz left, and I stared at the spreadsheets of red for a while, generally feeling sorry for myself. I took my sunglasses off and examined my eye using selfie mode on my phone. If anything, the bruise looked nastier now than it had that morning, the deep purple starting to turn blue and red at the edges.

I absently wondered if more makeup was a good idea as I checked my voicemail.

While I'd been hoping to have one from Vivienne's assistant with details about my one "big party," what I heard first was a local real estate agent who specialized in wine industry properties. Like Gene's investors, she could smell blood in the water, and asked if I was thinking of putting Oak Valley on the market. I had to admit, the price she quoted was tempting. I hit the button to save. Just in case.

I picked up the paper Schultz had left behind, forcing myself to read the article that went with the gruesome headline. It was another soliloquy by the prolific Bradley Wu. The food columnist who'd hailed my meal as "a culminating triumph of the baroque imagination," could now, apparently, only focus on one thing—death by Sirah. He'd worked in phrases like "dangerously deadly vineyard" and "hauntingly handsome young Adonis" to describe the deceased. Accurate if a bit flowery.

I skimmed down, spying a direct quote from David Allen. *"My Stepfather was a man of dangerous appetites. Am I surprised one finally came back to bite him? No."*

Hmm. It seemed Brad wasn't the only one with a flair for the dramatic.

I glossed over the rest of the article, unable to stop my mind from running through my list of suspects again. Of all the people who had been close to Chas, David seemingly had the best motive to keep him alive—Chas was consistently losing at poker to David and funneling money his way. That was, unless Chas'd had enough of being David's bankroller and decided to tell Mommy on him.

I grabbed my phone and scrolled through pictures of Chas's little black book again, going back over all the entries next to the initials D.A. By the time I'd added them all together, it looked like over the course of the last six months, Chas had owed David into the five figures. Significant. However, not significant enough for David to live off for long if Mommy cut him off for, say, gambling and bleeding her golden-boy husband dry. I thought of the way Vivienne had blamed herself for Chas's stealing. I could easily see her shifting that blame to David if she'd known he was the reason behind Chas's debt.

I put my hand to my temple, wondering where David Allen had been last night when I'd been whacked on the head.

I switched screens on my phone and dialed the home number for the Price-Pennington estate.

Four rings in, the deep voice of Lurch the Butler answered. "Price-Pennington residence."

"May I speak with David Allen please?"

There was a slight pause on the other end. "Mr. Allen has his own line in the guest residence."

Funny it was referred to as the guest residence and not David's residence. I wondered if that was intentional. "Would you happen to know the number?" I asked.

"I would."

I waited, rolling my eyes as silence stretched on. "Could you *give* it to me, please?"

"May I ask who is calling?" he countered instead.

"Emmy Oak. I was there earlier today," I added, hoping to jog his memory.

It must have worked, as he reluctantly rattled off the digits.

"Thank you," I told him, hanging up.

I dialed the number he'd given me, which rang on the other end. And rang. And rang. Six rings in, I got a generic recording telling me that the party had a voicemail box that was full and to try again.

I redialed the number of the main house instead.

"Price-Pennington Residence," came Lurch's answer.

"Hi, Emmy Oak here again," I told him.

I thought I detected a sigh on the other end, but I forged ahead.

"Listen, David doesn't seem to be answering his phone. Do you know if he's at home?"

"He is not."

I narrowed my eyes at the phone. "Then why did you just give me his home number?"

"You asked for it," came the monotone reply.

I gritted my teeth. "Do you know where he is?"

"I believe he is at the gallery. Now, if you will excuse me." He didn't wait for me to confirm or deny the excusing, as he hung up on me.

I remembered Ava saying she'd seen David exhibiting his work somewhere around town. I did a Google search and came up with the name of Salavence Gallery on 1st Street as the place to find his work currently on display. I noted the address, donned my sunglasses again, and grabbed my keys.

CHAPTER EIGHTEEN

Salavence Gallery was located in the trendy and touristy downtown area, just off E Napa Street. Sandwiched between an indie bookstore and a coffee shop, the storefront was all glass, several canvases showcasing modern art on display. I pushed through the doors, feeling the whoosh of air conditioning and hearing soft jazz music piped in through the speakers. The reception counter was a stark white lacquer, matching the white of the walls, floor, and ceiling. The entire place had a clinically blank feeling, making the art on the maze of walls scattered throughout the cavernous space pop under the bright overhead lights.

"May I help you?" asked a young woman behind the counter. In contrast to her surrounding, she was dressed in all black, sporting a severe black bob, long sleeved black blouse buttoned all the way up to her neck, and dark eye makeup that took the smoky look to the extreme.

"Hi. I, uh, was hoping to catch one of your artists here. David Allen?"

She nodded. "He's in the back. Installing his latest piece." She paused, giving me a quick up-and-down. "Are you a collector?"

"Maybe," I hedged. I had a feeling that in a place like this, I couldn't afford a postcard, let alone one of the 30" X 40" canvases.

She nodded, grabbing a pamphlet from behind the counter and handing it to me. "His show is next week. You can preview some of the pieces in the back, though." She gestured to the rear of the gallery.

I thanked her and headed through the maze of angled walls displaying various collections of work. Several different styles were represented, though most fell into the modern art category. I paused in front of one collection of landscapes done in abstract, thinking the artist had perfectly captured the warm hues of the Sonoma Valley during fall.

As I approached the back of the gallery, I heard two voices. One that I instantly recognized as David Allen's.

"I need more room. I have three more pieces that have to be in the show."

"Not possible," came the second voice. It was male as well, though high pitched with a nervous edge to it. "We agreed on six pieces. That's the limit."

I rounded the corner and spied the two men standing in front of a wall of the same type of artwork I'd seen in David's cottage. Lots of dark colors, violent strokes, and shapes that left the viewer with a general feeling of unease.

"I'm changing the agreement," David told the other man—a slim, well dressed guy with a twitch in his left eyebrow

"You cannot do that!" he shot back.

"Of course I can," came David's cool response. "I'm a Price."

The other man sputtered, but as he spied me, he shut his mouth with a click.

"Just move some of these other paintings," David continued. He looked up to see me, his face breaking into a smile that was less humor and more predatory. "Well, look who it is. Miss Wine and Die herself."

The second man looked perplexed, like he wasn't in on the joke.

"Emmy Oak," I offered, extending my hand.

He shook it, the name still not seeming to mean much to him. Good. At least this was one member of the public that hadn't heard about the Deadly Winery. I made a mental note to gloat about that to Schultz.

"Macklan Salavence," he told me. "Something I can help you with, Ms. Oak?" he asked, regaining his composure.

"I was hoping David could help me, actually."

David raised an eyebrow my way, the predatory grin spreading. Suddenly I was glad we were in a well-lit gallery and not a dark alley.

Or the dark pathway outside my cottage.

"Well, that sounds like a fun proposition," David said. Though it came out as more of a threat. Or maybe that was just my slightly concussed fear talking.

"I see," the gallery owner mumbled, retreating. "I'll, uh, just leave you two alone then."

I kinda wished he wouldn't, as David took a step closer to me.

Instinctively, I took one back.

"So, what can I do for you, Emmy?" he asked. His lips were still curved upward.

I cleared my throat, drawing courage from our brightly lit surroundings and the fact that two witnesses were in the building. "I was hoping you could tell me where you were last night."

His left eyebrow rose, and the corner of his mouth quirked up again. "I'm flattered you care so much about my nocturnal activities."

"Don't be." I laughed, but it sounded shaky even to my own ears. "Someone was trespassing at my winery last night."

"And you think I'm that hard up for a bottle of Chardonnay?"

"I think you might be desperate enough to threaten me."

For a half a second the smile dropped, and an intense emotion hit his eyes. A dark emotion, almost as unsettling as the painting he was standing in front of.

But just as quickly, he covered it, the mocking grin back. "Someone threatened you, huh? Is that what you're hiding behind these?" Before I could react, he lifted the sunglasses off my face. To his credit, he flinched slightly at the sight of my shiner. "Oh, Emmy. Ouch."

"No kidding," I said, grabbing my glasses back from his hand.

"And you think *I* did this?" David tsked between his teeth and shook his head. "I'm hurt, Emmy. You must know I hold you in much too high a regard for that."

While it was phrased as a compliment, something about the hint of sarcasm creeping into his voice made it difficult to fully believe.

"I know Chas owed you money," I told him.

If he was surprised by my knowledge, he didn't show it, his cool demeanor remaining in place. "Pity I won't be able to collect now."

"Did he threaten to tell your mother that you were bleeding him dry?"

"Why would he do that?" David asked.

Which I noticed did not directly answer my question.

"Maybe he was desperate. He'd been borrowing from a loan shark to pay his debts."

David paused. "So you've met Trask."

I nodded. "And I know Chas was in over his head. Did he threaten to tell Vivienne everything to get her to bail him out?"

His gaze met mine. "That looks painful," he said, changing the subject as he gestured to my black eye. "I assume you didn't get a good look at the person who did this?"

I paused. "I saw enough," I bluffed, hoping to tip his hand into a confession.

He stared for a beat, and I felt like I was in a silent game of chicken.

Finally he turned to his painting, his expression hidden from me. "Then you know I didn't do it."

"Where were you?" I asked again, realizing he hadn't answered my original question.

"Home," he said, his eyes on the painting, hands shifting the left corner just slightly higher, making minuscule adjustments.

"Your mother can vouch for that, I suppose?"

David shrugged. "I don't know. I didn't see her."

"Your grandmother?"

"Sorry. I didn't kiss Granny good night either."

"So you were alone?"

David turned his sharklike smile my way, showing off a row of teeth. "I didn't say that, now, did I?"

"So you do have an alibi?"

"You make it sound so dramatic, Ems."

The mocking tone was back. I wondered if it was David's brand of flirting. If so, I couldn't imagine the type of lady who might have followed him back to his cottage last night.

"Being knocked unconscious *was* dramatic," I countered.

Something flickered behind his eyes again. "I hope you catch whoever did it."

"I intend to," I told him, with a lot more gusto and bravery than I felt.

* * *

While I'd hoped to get more from David—like at least the name of the girl he'd supposedly been with last night—I figured the alibi would be easy enough to check out. While the cottage was at the back of the property, there was only the main drive in from the road. Someone must have seen him coming or going. That is, if he was my attacker.

I turned that thought over as I drove home, picturing the dark, explosive emotions I'd seen behind his eyes. David had a prescription for Xanax. He hadn't denied that Chas was threatening to go to Vivienne about the poker games, David's winnings, and the debt. Not only was David's cash cow looking to default on his debt, but he was also threatening to cut off any allowance from Mommy. I had a hard time believing David could live in the manner to which he'd become accustomed on an artist's income. If my theory was right, Chas stood to destroy David's way of life.

If.

That was the problem. I had lots of good theories but no evidence to take them from the realm of *if* to putting the killer behind bars.

I pulled up the gravel drive and parked in the lot, trying not to be depressed at the distinct lack of cars there. I made my way into the main kitchen and began pulling ingredients. Olive oil, onion, a dry white wine, parmesan cheese. Cooking always cleared my head, and I hoped for the same sort of clarity now as all the jumbled bits and pieces of information I had about Chas flew around in my brain without seeming to fit together anywhere. Besides, I had a memorial to cater the next day, and this was a chance to make a better impression on the society set—a set I sorely hoped had many less somber occasions they'd like to book our winery for in the future.

I settled on a menu of two different savory dishes with wine pairings, and a few plates of fruits, cheeses, and mini cheesecakes and cookies for dessert. For the first savory bite, I grabbed a filet mignon from the refrigerator and seasoned it. My plan was a quick sear, then thinly slice it to top a layer of blue cheese on crostini. A quick garnish of fresh herbs and balsamic vinegar at the last minute would be all it needed to be a delicious, elegant bite. As I'd mentioned to Vivienne, it would pair perfectly with our Pinot Noir.

For the second dish, I settled on a Truffle Risotto Bite, fried in an arancini-style to make for an easy-to-eat appetizer. I'd be able to make the risotto base ahead of time, then fry them on site, just before the party, so they'd stay warm and crispy.

I grabbed the arborio rice and chicken stock, getting the stock heating while I chopped onions and garlic. The rhythmic movements of the knife and homey scent of chicken broth heating on the stove put me in my zone, blocking out the rest of the world in a warm, steamy cocoon of comfort. I worked quietly, stirring the liquid ladle by ladle into the rice until it had a creamy consistency. Then I added parmesan and the truffle oil before setting it aside to cool. I did a small test batch of fried bites, rolling the risotto into little balls, coating in breadcrumbs, and dropping them in the deep fryer. They only took a couple of minutes before they came out a golden brown. I barely let one cool before my growling stomach forced me to dig in.

The outside was a perfectly crispy crunch, while the inside was decadently creamy. I closed my eyes, leaning my head back as I let the earthy flavor of the truffles mix with the sharp tang of the parmesan on my tongue. This was heaven in one little bite. I think I might have moaned slightly.

"Wow, must be good."

My eyes snapped open, my body tensing and my hand instinctively reaching for the chef's knife on the cutting board. Only as I focused through the surge of adrenaline, it was not an intruder who stood in my kitchen doorway but Detective Grant.

His eyes went to the knife in my hand. "Jumpy?"

I narrowed my own eyes at him. "As one is when they've recently been attacked." I set the knife down with a clatter. "Geez, you almost gave me a heart attack."

"Sorry," he said, his voice softer, as if he really meant it. Some of my anger melted. "I just wanted to check in on you," he went on.

Dang it. The rest of the anger fell away as his dark eyes made a slow sweep of the bruises I'd been hiding all day.

"Thanks," I said. "I'm fine."

"Yeah, you look great." The corner of his mouth ticked upward.

I returned it with a self-deprecating, "I look like a raccoon who let a two-year-old do her eye makeup."

He laughed, the sound rich and deep. The sudden transformation in him surprised me almost as much as his sudden presence. "Well, at least your sense of humor is unharmed." He gestured to the risotto balls on the counter. "Mind if I try one?"

I pushed the platter toward him.

He grabbed one, the crunch audible as he bit in. I found myself watching his expression carefully—purely for professional reasons of course. His eyes fluttered closed for a second, his mouth going slack as he chewed. "Wow. That's good," he practically moaned.

"Thanks." I couldn't help the lift of pride in my voice.

"These for a party?" he asked, gesturing to the large batch of risotto still cooling on the counter.

"Sort of. Chas Pennington's memorial tomorrow." I paused. "I don't suppose there are any new developments?"

Some of the ease left Grant's face at the mention, and I almost wished I'd kept my big mouth shut. "I can't discuss an ongoing investigation."

Rats. "Okay, what about this—any luck finding the creep who attacked me last night?"

"No." His jaw clenched. "But I will."

I almost felt sorry for said creep. Grant looked like he was ready to destroy him.

I decided to switch gears. "I promise wine country isn't always this exciting."

He gave me a questioning look.

"You did move to Sonoma for a slower pace, right?"

Grant paused, popped another bite into his mouth, and chewed thoughtfully. Finally he said, "Right. Slower pace."

I watched him. "That's not the whole reason, though, is it?"

His eyes met mine, and I could tell I was right. The gold flecks darkened, almost as if they were hiding like the secret he was protecting. "Let's just say the change of pace wasn't entirely my idea."

So this *was* a demotion. "What happened?" I asked, wondering how far I could press this easier side of him before it dissolved into Tough Guy again.

He took a deep breath in, his nostril flaring with the effort. "I suppose it's public record. There was a shooting. Internal affairs got involved. When it was all over, they felt it best if I moved to a new venue."

I digested that, trying to read between the sparsely filled lines. "You shot someone?"

He nodded slowly, his eyes dark. And filled with a cocktail of emotion I couldn't begin to interpret. I could imagine a healthy dose of guilt lay there, but whether it was tempered with regret or anger, I couldn't say.

"When was this?" I asked.

"Last year."

"I'm sorry." As soon as I said the words, I wanted to take them back. I could tell by the way his expression tightened that Tough Guy didn't do sympathy. "I mean, I'm sorry you had to move here. It's got to be a lot less exciting than San Francisco."

He tilted his head in concession. "There are some benefits, though."

"Oh?"

He grinned, grabbing another risotto ball, and tossed it into his mouth. "These, for one."

While it wasn't the compliment I'd been hoping for, I'd take it. "Thanks. But save some for the guests, huh?"

CHAPTER NINETEEN

Morning dawned much too early on Thursday, sunlight smacking me in the face after another restless night of tossing, turning—this one full of images of David Allen, Vivienne, and Sadie all coming after me with rocks in hand. I tore myself from my warm blankets and stumbled to the bathroom to shower.

Luckily, the reassuring bathroom mirror told me my black eye was fading, and I was able to cover most of it with makeup. At least well enough that I wouldn't have to attend the memorial in dark sunglasses. I dressed in a simple little black dress and low heels that were stylish while still affording me pain-free movement for circulating between the guests and the kitchen.

Conchita and Hector helped me load my Wrangler with trays and equipment, the overflow going in the trunk of Conchita's Camry. Jean Luc rode with me, and Ava had agreed to meet us there to act as my serving help for the afternoon. Per the instructions Vivienne's assistant had left on my voicemail, we drove around to the Links service entrance at the back of the club, where we were directed to the kitchen and the large clubroom where the reception would take place after the service. It was a comfortable room, adorned in tastefully solemn flowers, deep burgundy cloths draped over tables, and a small grouping of armchairs in dim lighting. Along the right wall the staff had set up a long table for us to lay out finger foods and desserts, and a bar stood in the corner where Jean Luc could pour drinks for the guests. He quickly began setting up there, uncorking and decanting the Pinot Noir and chilling the Chardonnay we'd brought for the occasion.

Near the back of the room sat a small table draped in black. A large wreath had been placed on it, behind a heavy looking bronze urn, which I assumed contained the earthly remains of the late Chas Pennington. As much as my opinion of the man fell with each detail of his life I stumbled upon, I felt a pang of sorrow at the finality of the scene. I tried to shake it off, focusing on the job at hand.

Ava stayed behind in the clubroom to help Jean Luc set up, and Conchita and I spent the next hour frying, preparing, and arranging artful presentations on our canapé trays. We had most of them ready by the time the memorial started at two. I left Conchita to the finishing touches and slipped into the back of the functions room where the service was being held.

I immediately spied a somberly dressed Vivienne in the front row, a tissue clutched to her nose. David Allen sat on one side of her and the stoic Alison Price on the other. Needless to say, neither was looking likely to need a tissue that day—David wearing his bored smirk and Alison staring straight ahead with about as much emotion as if she were here to watch a golf match and not bury her son-in-law.

Across the aisle from them sat Jenny with an older couple I took to be her parents. Her mother was an aged, plumper version of Jenny, and the man was tall, with a weathered face that looked like it had seen its fair share of time in the elements. His shoulders stooped slightly, and he coughed into a handkerchief intermittently. Both looked drained, as if the sheer act of sitting upright in a crowded room was almost more than their bodies could bear. I felt a wave of sympathy toward the couple.

The rest of the room was populated with men in suits and women in tasteful dark colored dresses and slacks. I recognized a few faces from my previous trip to the Links, one or two who had been on the Spanish party's guest list, and the distinct profile of Sadie Evans, sitting halfway back in a sharp black pinstripe suit and a little hat with feathers.

The service itself was short and sweet—no long-winded, heartfelt eulogies. A few words were said by a man I assumed to be Vivienne's pastor, offering hope and consolation to the bereaved. I noticed quite a few women in the crowd letting out quiet tears and suddenly wondered how many *mistakes* Chas had really made. Sadie's eyes, I noticed, were bone dry. Either she had long ago checked all emotion at the door where Chas was concerned, or she was a great faker. Then again, she'd been practically brought up in the boardroom. Maybe Sadie Evans just didn't do emotion.

Music began to play, and the crowd to disperse to pay respects, which I took as my cue to leave, making my way ahead of the crowd to the clubroom to check that we were ready for the onslaught.

Conchita had assembled the blue cheese filet crostini, and was just adding the chopped chives and microgreens. Beside those, truffle risotto bites were laid out on long, elegant white plates, nestled in a bed of fresh sage leaves and spring greens. Everything looked perfect and delicious.

I had just finished adding small wooden toothpicks to the risotto bites for easy handling, when I saw Vivienne and her entourage enter the room.

She stood at the door, receiving hugs, handshakes, and air kisses from the mourners as they filed in. David Allen stood a beat behind her, not, I noticed, greeting anyone. He was wearing his usually sullen expression, though his eyes looked heavy and lidded. I wondered if he'd popped a Xanax before the memorial. It certainly might help calm the nerves…especially if he'd been the one to put Chas in that urn in the first place.

Alison Price stood tall at her daughter's side as part of the greeting line, murmuring to guests as they arrived. While I could just make out mumbled words of sympathy, her eyes held absolutely none of the sentiments she expressed. She looked as if she was going through the motions of polite society but couldn't wait for the final send-off to be over.

Sadie Evans made her way through the line, stiffly air kissing Vivienne. She leaned in and whispered something to the older woman, which had the lines around Vivienne's mouth drawing down into a deep frown. Vivienne's eyes followed Sadie even as she walked away, making her way to the table with the urn, ostensibly to admire the flowers.

I watched the tense exchange, wondering just what Sadie had said. Had it been about the affair? The stolen company funds? The gambling debts?

"Everything is lovely." Jenny Pacheco was suddenly at my side. "Thank you for this."

"Of course." I gave her a quick hug. "How are you holding up?"

She shrugged. "Well, I survived jail." She gave me a wry grin.

I shook my head. "Jenny, I'm so sorry. Believe me—I'm doing everything I can to convince the police of your innocence."

She nodded. "I know. And really, you've done so much already. I-I really can't thank you enough."

I shook my head. "No need to. You'd do the same for me." I paused, looking across the room to where her parents were standing over the bronze urn now, both tearing. "I'm glad they could make it."

Jenny nodded. "Mom wants me to come back to Arizona with them." She paused. "But the lawyer said I have to stay in town. Condition of my bail."

She looked so small and fragile that my heart went out to her. That someone should be dealing with the scary prospect of a lifetime in jail while also working through the grief of losing a loved one just wasn't fair. I was suddenly angry at Grant all over again for arresting her.

Jenny excused herself to be with her parents, and I circulated among the guests, watching Ava do the same on the other side of the room, making sure everyone had a full glass and ample opportunity to sample the hors d'oeuvres. While the mood of the gathering was subdued, the snippets of conversation I caught seemed to be positive about the food and wine pairings. I held on to that cheery thought as Sadie Evans approached me, a half empty glass of Pinot in hand.

"This is good," she told me, gesturing to the glass. "Yours?"

I nodded. "It's a fickle grape to grow, but worth it. I love the subtle blackberry notes."

Sadie sipped her glass again. "It's nice. Not too brash."

I tried not to laugh at the pot calling the glass brash. "Thanks. I'd be happy to supply you with a case if you'd like. We have several set aside."

She nodded. "I just might. Maybe a case of that Petite Sirah Chas raved about too."

I froze, her words sinking in. Along with the implications of that seemingly simple statement. Chas Pennington had only just tasted the Sirah at the Spanish party. The party Sadie had *not* been at. When had he had time to rave?

"You spoke to Chas while he was at the party?" I asked carefully.

Sadie gave me a blank stare, as if the implication of what she'd just said was slow to set in for her as well. "I…I…y-yes. I suppose I did."

"You were there?" I pushed, feeling bold in the security of the crowded room.

Sadie licked her lips, eyes darting to Vivienne, who stood near the urn, sniffling into a tissue. "Look, Viv doesn't need to know this, okay?"

"You *were* there." This time it was a statement, not a question.

"Yes," she hissed in a whisper. "Yes, okay, I was there. Briefly." She glanced in Vivienne's direction again.

"When?" I asked, mentally running down the timeline Grant had given me for the drugs being introduced into Chas's system.

"Just after Chas arrived. He called me. We…we'd had an argument before he left for the party."

"About him stalling in asking Vivienne for a divorce?"

Her skin paled a shade under her makeup. "H-how did you know about that?"

"Lucky guess," I said, glossing over it so as not to out Jenny's eavesdropping. "So you were pressuring Chas to leave Vivienne?"

"No, you have it all wrong," she said, shaking her head. "It was Chas's idea. He promised me he'd leave her." She paused. "But then he…well, he said the timing just wasn't right yet."

If I had to guess, Chas never had any intention of leaving his sugar mama. He'd been stringing Sadie along with false promises, just like everyone else in his life.

"So what happened after you argued?" I asked her.

"Chas left for the party, but then he called and said he was sorry. He said he needed to see me. It was urgent."

"What did he want?"

Sadie threw her hands up. "I don't know! I never saw him."

I narrowed my eyes at her. "You mean to tell me that you drove all the way to Sonoma to talk to Chas, just to turn around and go home?"

She leaned in closer, her tone confidential. "Look, Chas said he wanted to see me. You don't understand the kind of draw that guy had. He was magnetic, you know?"

No I didn't. But I did know he was dead, and Sadie suddenly had opportunity along with motive. "What happened when you got to Oak Valley?"

Sadie sighed. "I called him, but he didn't pick up. I waited, tried again. Finally he texted me saying he couldn't get away from Viv after all. He thought she suspected something and was sticking to him like glue. Said she just kept pouring him more Sirah. I waited a few more minutes to see if he could shake her. Then I got sick of it and went home. End of story."

Or at least the end of the story she was telling me. "I thought you said you had broken up with Chas."

Sadie sucked in her cheeks, sizing me up. "I did." She paused. "But he was hard to say no to."

I wondered. It was possible she was telling the truth and she'd fallen under the boy wonder's spell. It was also just as likely she'd driven to Oak Valley not for a liaison with Chas but to put an end to his stringing her along.

Or possibly to his stealing from her company funds.

"Did you know about Chas's corporate expense requests?" I asked, watching her reaction carefully.

If she had one, she hid it well, her expression not changing. Either that or she'd had a lot of Botox done recently. "What about them?" she asked.

I shrugged. "Nothing," I said. "I just heard he had a lot of them." If she already knew about Chas's theft, she wasn't letting on. And if she didn't, I figured that was Vivienne's business.

Sadie waved me off. "The man had expensive taste. I'm sure accounting vetted them all."

"I'm sure," I murmured. I spied Vivienne accepting a canapé from Ava, then moving through the crowd. She caught my eye and made her way toward us, her mother a vigilant step behind her.

Sadie must have noticed as well, as she took that as her cue to move on, mumbling that she'd contact me about that case of Pinot Noir later. I hoped she meant it.

"Emmy, this is all lovely. Thank you," Vivienne said through a teary smile as she approached.

"Glad I could help," I told her.

"I'm sure Chas would have approved," she went on, nodding as she surveyed the room.

I thought I heard Alison snort behind her daughter, but she was lady enough to cover it quickly.

"He seems to have a lot of friends here," I said, trying not to let my gaze fall on the several mourning women in attendance.

Vivienne nodded. "He was very well liked."

"*You* are well liked, darling," Alison corrected her daughter. "They are here to support you."

Vivienne frowned. "Not everyone shares your opinion of Chas."

While I had to agree that Alison's remarks might be harsh, she was probably more right than Vivienne on this one. Save for the weeping ladies' club, I had a feeling not many people in the room were actually mourning Chas's passing. In fact, I thought, as I spied David Allen near the bar, there was a very good chance one of them had even facilitated it.

"I was wondering," I said, approaching the subject carefully, "if either of you happened to see David the night before last?"

Vivienne blinked at me, trying to ascertain my meaning. "Tuesday? I-I don't know." She glanced at her mother as if looking to her for the answer.

"What did David do?" Alison asked, narrowing her eyes.

"Nothing," I lied. "I just thought I saw him somewhere, but I may have been mistaken. Was he at home?"

"I wouldn't know," Alison said, eyes still narrow, as if she wasn't buying my vague explanation. "David lives in the guest cottage. He keeps his own hours."

"I think I saw his car Monday," Vivienne said, still trying to recall. "But really, the days have all kind of blurred together. It's just been so hard without Chas." She sniffled again, reaching for her tissue.

I thought I caught Alison roll her eyes, but she covered it so quickly that I wasn't sure.

"Does David have a girlfriend?" I asked, feeling his alibi for the night of my attack growing weaker by the second.

"David?" Alison said. "Oh, I'd be highly surprised."

Vivienne sniffled louder. "He's all I have left."

Alison's features softened, and she put a strong arm around her daughter's shoulders. "You have me. Come on, let's get you a drink." She nodded in my direction before leading her daughter to Jean Luc's capable hands.

I watched their retreating backs, wondering at Vivienne's last words. Despite their strained relationship, she clearly loved her son. Did she love him enough to be willing to cover for David Allen? He was her child, but if she knew he'd killed Chas, would that be enough to sever the tie? Or would she cling to her one remaining heir even tighter?

"Emmy."

I looked up to find Conchita hailing me from the doorway with another tray of crostini. I quickly crossed the room to relieve her of it, swapping it out for an empty one.

The rest of the memorial went smoothly, the subdued conversations and mumbled sympathies continuing until most of our trays were empty and we'd gone through two cases of both Chardonnay and the Pinot Noir. As the sun began to sink behind the hills, the mourners dispersed slowly—some of the Links members going toward the bar and lounge, while others made their way toward the valet for their cars. Cleanup was fairly easy, considering we'd done the bulk of the prep at the winery. Conchita, Ava, and I gathered chafing dishes, tidied the clubroom, and tried to leave everything as clean, if not cleaner, than we'd found it.

As we cleared the remains of the memorial, I couldn't help my mind rolling over all of the attendees who'd had reason to want the guest of honor dead.

David Allen still held a place as my favorite, his precarious position with Mommy Moneybags feeling like motive enough to want his stepfather out of the picture. If Vivienne had found out David was the reason Chas was visiting loan sharks and stealing from Price Digital, I could well see her kicking David out of her guest house as well as her will. Not to mention, David had a handy prescription for Xanax.

But then there was Vivienne herself. While she played the grieving widow well, Chas had played *her* well enough that she had plenty to be angry with him over. He'd cheated on her, squandered her money, and stolen from her company. That was enough to break any relationship. And what had Sadie said about the party—that Vivienne was sticking to Chas like glue? Maybe she'd been sticking close not because she suspected he was planning a liaison with another woman but because she was waiting for the perfect opportunity to spike his wine.

Of course that brought me to Sadie herself. While she'd been in the back of my mind ever since we'd learned of Chas's infidelity, she'd seemingly had no opportunity to administer the lethal dose. Knowing now that she was actually at the winery during the time Chas had been poisoned, suddenly painted her in a whole new light. And I could easily imagine no-nonsense Sadie poisoning her former-lover-turned-embezzler without blinking a false eyelash.

And as much as the people in Chas's personal life all seemed to be better off without him, there was also the possibility his death had nothing to do with lovers or liaisons and everything to do with an unpaid debt to a ruthless loan shark. It wasn't a stretch to imagine Joe Trask could have threatened another debtor to slip a little something into Chas's drink. Heck, in that scenario, it was even possible the guilty party hadn't even known what he was putting in Chas's drink or that it would result in his death.

My mind ran over and over all the possible scenarios as I stepped outside with the last armload of chafing dishes to deposit into Conchita's trunk before we left.

The clouds had come rolling in while we'd been inside saying our last goodbyes to Chas Pennington, and the sky was dark. A fine mist permeated the air, threatening real rain later. I fumbled with the key fob to Conchita's Camry, wrangling the trunk open. I was just setting down my load when footsteps sounded on the gravel behind me.

I hoped I hadn't left something behind. I spun around expecting to find Jean Luc rushing up with a stray bottle of Pinot he'd rescued from a fate in the trash bin.

But instead all I saw was a large, indistinguishable object rushing toward my face.

And then nothing but blackness.

CHAPTER TWENTY

My first thought when I awoke was that I'd been buried alive. I tried to sit up and hit my head against something hard just inches above me. I pushed with my cramped legs, but I could only partially straighten them before they came up against a solid wall. Panic collected in my chest, suddenly making it hard to breathe as I furiously blinked in the darkness. Had someone put me in Chas's coffin instead of the deceased? Was I being lowered into the ground? Had I already been buried?

I forced myself to take slow breaths, focusing. No, Chas was in an urn. He'd been cremated. There had been no casket. So where was I?

I explored with my fingers in the pitch black, ignoring the headache blooming behind my eyes. I remembered being hit on the head…the second time this week. And it was no more pleasant now. I forced myself to focus through the pain. The floor felt…fuzzy? And it was vibrating. No, not just vibrating—moving.

I strained to think back. The last thing I remembered I was standing outside Conchita's car before I'd been hit. It dawned on me. I was in Conchita's trunk.

And someone was driving.

My attacker? Panic surged through me anew at that thought. Where was he taking me? To dump me for dead somewhere? Or worse…to make *sure* I was dead somewhere?

I shifted, trying to turn over and use my right hand, currently pinned beneath me. I could only wiggle it in the cramped interior, rendering it virtually useless. I reached my left hand up, feeling above me on the trunk's lid for an emergency latch. Unfortunately, it had been years since Conchita had bought a new car, and hers was pre emergency release. Nothing I could get a grip on moved or budged the lid an inch.

I resisted the urge to cry out for help—knowing the only person likely to hear me was the one who'd put me there.

I crawled my fingers along the floor, feeling for anything I could use as a weapon. But all I came up against were the chafing dishes I'd been loading before being rendered unconscious. I silently cursed my bad luck as I felt a cramp in my side. If only I'd been loading in something smaller, I'd have more room. Canapé plates would have been nice.

I closed my eyes, wondering how long I'd been out. How far had my attacker driven already? For all I knew, we could be around the block from the Links or several miles out into vineyards and farmland. Acres upon acres of dark, isolated landscape where it would likely be days before anyone found my body.

I gave myself a mental shake, refusing to think that way. I would find a way out of this. I had to. The winery needed me. Conchita and Hector. Mom. They all depended on me.

I held on to that thought, holding back the hot tears I could feel trying to make their way down my cheeks in the claustrophobic interior.

I'm not sure how much time passed. It felt like hours in the tiny space with only my thoughts of the worst case scenario to keep me company. In reality, it could have easily only been minutes. But finally the car turned, sending me sliding backward into a half empty box of napkins. Then bumpy terrain ensued, jostling me so hard I thought every bone in my body would be bruised. By the time we finally stopped, I was filled with a mix of relief and fear, wondering just what to expect next.

I strained in the darkness, hearing a car door open and shut. Footsteps. Heavy breathing. I tensed, instinctively curling my fingers around a chafing dish lid—the closest thing to a weapon I could find.

One that, as it turned out, would do me little good.

As the trunk lid opened, I was greeted with the shiny muzzle of a gun pointed right at me.

The cold air hit me like a punch, followed by pure fear at the sight of the gun.

"Get out."

I forced my eyes away from the gun muzzle to the person who was holding it straight-armed at me. And all emotion gave way to just one—confusion.

Alison Price.

"Get out," she commanded again, her voice hard and direct. Even if she hadn't been pointing a gun at me, I'd have been tempted to comply.

I slowly set the chafing dish lid down and climbed out of the trunk, unfolding my cramped limbs with some difficulty.

"Mrs. Price," I croaked out, hearing the hitch of fear in my own voice. "What is going on?"

"You're a smart girl," she shot back. "You figure it out."

I licked my lips, wishing she hadn't thought I was so smart. Truthfully, I was feeling pretty dumb right about now.

"Okay." I paused, jumping ahead several conclusions. "You killed Chas Pennington."

"Bravo," she said, though there was no emotion in the word, least of all praise. "See, I knew you were too smart."

Up until that moment, I hadn't been. My "smart" money had been on David Allen.

"But why?" I asked. Not that I cared that much anymore. What I cared about was keeping her talking. Prolonging whatever plans she had until someone could find me.

I glanced around. As I'd guessed, we were in a vineyard. Where, I had no idea. Mountains rose to the right, but other than that, no landmarks were visible in the darkness. How long had we been driving? And how long would it take for anyone to realize I was gone? Surely someone would see Conchita's car missing, but I had a sinking feeling that finding it would prove more of a challenge.

"Why did you kill Chas?" I asked again.

"Why?" Alison repeated, her tone mocking. "Surely you've been nosing around our family enough to know the answer to that. The man was a leech. A criminal. A drain on everyone he met. And I would not have him taking my daughter down with him."

"So, you knew about the illegal poker games?" I surmised.

She nodded.

"How did you find out?"

"David," she spat out.

That surprised me. "David told you?" I hadn't gotten the impression he was close enough to his grandmother for confidences like that.

But she barked out laughter. "Please. That boy couldn't tell a truthful tale if his life depended on it. I had him followed."

I blinked, trying to keep up. "You hired someone to follow your grandson?"

She shrugged. "Brackston was happy to do it."

The name meant nothing to me, which must have shown on my face as she clarified, "Our butler."

Oh! Lurch. "Why did you have Lur—uh, Brackston follow your grandson?"

"I thought he was doing drugs."

Good instincts. Though, in California at least, what David was smoking wasn't illegal.

"I thought if I could prove it, I could have Vivienne force him into rehab."

"You wanted to help him," I asked, trying to see a smidgen of heart in the suddenly cold eyes staring back at me.

She gave that bark of humorless laughter again. "I wanted him away from my daughter. He was almost as much of a drain on her as Chas—emotionally and financially. You know he's almost thirty years old and has never held down a job?"

"I thought he was an artist."

Her eye narrowed. "I mean a *real* job."

Ouch. While his art wasn't my taste, I could tell he was good. At least, Ava had said he was, and I trusted her opinion.

Ava. My throat clogged at the thought of her. Would I ever see her again? Ever be able to have a *Thelma & Louise* night over rocky road? I forced back tears, concentrating on what Alison was saying. I had to stay focused if I had any chance of getting out of this alive.

"…dragging my daughter down. She was capable of so much. And all they did was take, take, take."

"Like Chas?" I asked, getting her back on track.

She paused, her grip on the gun going tighter until I could see blue veins straining against her pale skin. I instinctively took a step back, feeling the back of my knees hitting up against the car fender.

"Like Chas," she confirmed.

"So, Brackston followed David to a poker game," I said, drawing out the tale as long as I could.

She nodded. "Brackston talked to a couple of people and found out Chas was the one setting up the games. Not only that, but he was losing. Losing my daughter's money."

"So you killed him?"

"Oh, I'm not a barbarian." Her spine straightened in defense. "I talked to Chas first. Gave him a chance to leave quietly on his own."

"But he refused?" Which came as no surprise. Why would Chas leave? He had the perfect setup. A wife with deep pockets and a blind eye.

Alison confirmed my suspicions, shaking her head. "No. That smug slime just laughed at me. He said Vivienne would never believe me. That he had her wrapped around his little finger. Can you believe the gall of that man? I'm her *mother*."

I swallowed hard, trying to find anything even slightly maternal about the way that gun was aimed so steadily at my heart. "So what happened then?"

Alison's features darkened, her jaw tightening. "Then he told me just how blind my daughter was to his activities. He said he had his hands in her money and she didn't even know it."

"The company funds," I concluded.

Alison nodded slowly. "See, I knew you knew too much."

If only I had. If only I'd been able to put it together sooner and tell Grant. Or Schultz and his lawyers. Or anyone who might come looking for me now.

I scanned the dark vineyard, hearing nothing but my own breath as a light rain began to fall.

No one was coming. It was me versus Alison. And while I might have her by a good forty years, she was taller, sturdy, and had a gun. Not odds I'd guess even Chas would have bet on.

"What did you do then?" I asked, desperately trying to stall until some magical escape plan came to me.

Alison shrugged. "What could I do? The gambling was one thing. But embezzling from her company? Vivienne could have lost everything if that had gotten out."

"So you killed him."

"It was surprisingly easy, really," she said, her eyes going far away, as if reliving it. "I took it upon myself to order a refill of David's prescription. It's all online these days, you know," she added. "Makes it quite easy and convenient to do. Especially if you know all of the patient's personal info. No one at the pharmacy even blinked an eye when I told them I was picking up my grandson's prescription for him."

"So they were David's pills that killed Chas—not Jenny's?"

Alison nodded. "Unfortunately, the police pinned it on that girl." She shrugged. "But sacrifices have to be made."

Anger pricked the back of my throat at the idea Jenny's freedom was a sacrifice Alison was willing to make. "She could get life in prison."

"She was never going to amount to anything anyway. Look at her. She couldn't even keep an entry level job at Price Digital."

"That's because Chas had her fired!" I blurted out in Jenny's defense.

Alison raised one pale eyebrow in a perfect arch, her mouth curving into a smile. "Really? His own sister? Well, you see the man really didn't have any redeeming qualities. I did the world a favor."

I had a feeling a few people would agree with her, but that didn't negate the fact she'd taken a life. Or that she was holding a gun on me. I took a shallow breath, reining in my emotion.

"Why did you choose Xanax to kill Chas?" I asked.

"Well, I knew Chas took them. On the sly." She paused. "He did other drugs too, you know."

That, I did know. But I figured now was not the time to strengthen my smarty-pants image in her eyes. "Oh?" I asked.

She nodded. "Cocaine. His tramp, Sadie Evans, got him hooked. I'd seen him coming home at all hours, high as a kite. Then he'd take his sister's Xanax to come down before facing Viv." She shook her head. "I almost thought I could just wait it out. With the dangerous cocktail he was taking, it was only a matter of time before he offed himself."

"But you didn't want to wait?"

Alison slowly shook her head. "I couldn't. He was going to ruin Vivienne. And I saw my chance with your party at the winery. Vivienne told me Chas would be driving in from the city from work—which I knew meant he was getting high with his tramp. Of course, he'd need to come down before the party, taking a couple Xanax. And I knew how Chas liked to drink. By the third glass, he wouldn't have blinked an eye at a slightly bitter taste in his Sirah." She paused again, a slow, wicked smile snaking across her face. "In fact, he didn't blink an eye. He just drank up."

And died in my cellar.

I shivered in the damp cold enveloping us. As much as Chas Pennington hadn't been much of a humanitarian, no one deserved to die that way.

"What about Vivienne?" I asked. "Didn't you think she'd be devastated?"

Alison narrowed her eyes at me, taking a step forward. "My daughter is my whole life. I've worked hard to give her every advantage. I've invested so much in that girl, made so many sacrifices. And then what does she do? She squanders her life on one worthless deadbeat after another."

The fire in Alison's eyes was enough to scare the bejesus out of me, even if it hadn't had the power of a pistol behind it. As her monologue went on, I put my right hand behind my back, feeling along the rear of the car for anything I could use as a weapon against the increasingly agitated woman.

"Lord knows, her first husband was no saint," she told me. "But I took care of him quickly enough."

"Wait—took care?" I asked, suddenly wondering if Vivienne's first husband was in a bronze urn somewhere too.

Alison smiled. "Relax, dear. He's alive and well. Well, alive anyway. Might have been more *well* if my daughter hadn't caught him with a prostitute and invoked the infidelity clause of their prenup. She left him with nothing." Her eyes were dark and hard again. "Bubbles was her name. Best hundred dollars I ever spent."

I blinked, realizing just how unhinged Alison was. I was sure Vivienne had no idea her mother had broken up her first marriage. And she'd kept this secret all these years.

"But Pennington," she went on, taking another step closer.

I cringed as that muzzle was getting way too close for comfort. My fingers scrambled behind me, coming up against only smooth, firmly attached chrome.

"Pennington was low rent," Alison continued. "A big step down for her. I was mortified when she announced their engagement. His father was a farmworker, for Pete's sake. I told her he was just a gold digger. But she wouldn't listen." Alison shook her head. "She was always like that, even as a girl. So stubborn. So, I had to step in."

Like I feared she was stepping in now. Panic was building in my chest again, making my hands shake. I had to find a way out. And fast.

"How did you get the Xanax into Chas's glass unnoticed?" I asked, not caring about the answer so much as prolonging the inevitable.

"I simply crushed a few tablets." She paused. "Maybe more than a few. But I wanted to make sure they did the trick. No comfortable comas for Chas Pennington. He needed to be really, truly gone."

I personally didn't see anything terrifically comfortable about a coma caused by drug overdose, but I didn't interrupt.

"I made sure to wear my gloves that day—perfectly appropriate for an afternoon garden party, wouldn't you say?"

I nodded. I had to concede, I hadn't thought a thing about it at the time.

"All the better to keep prints off the glasses. I poured myself a glass of the Sirah, then slipped into the ladies' room with it and emptied the Xanax powder into the glass. It changed the color just slightly, but after stirring it with a straw, it was close enough that I knew my inebriated son-in-law wouldn't notice."

"And you just handed him the tainted wine?"

"Everybody was going from table to table, socializing. I found Chas sitting alone at the family table. His speech was already slurred when I handed it to him. Told him Vivienne poured it for him."

So Jenny's prints on the glass had really been an accident. I could easily see her touching it at the family's table, maybe even to move it further from her brother's reach as the night wore on and he became increasingly drunk.

"You didn't worry about anyone finding the glass later?" I asked.

"Why would I?" she said, her forehead creasing in a frown. "No one could trace anything back to me. The prescription was David's. The wineglass wasn't mine. And the Sirah was yours, dear." She flashed that wicked smile at me again, and I felt a surge of anger that she was fine with me and Oak Valley playing scapegoat in her plan.

"Was it you who hit me on the head too?" I asked, anger making me bold.

She shook her head, tsking between her teeth. "Brackston was happy to help me with that little problem. As soon as you mentioned the name of that greedy little pawnbroker to me at the Links, I knew you were in danger of getting too close. At least to knowing about Vivienne covering Chas's embezzling. Imagine if her board had gotten hold of that? Not to mention that vampire, Sadie Evans."

She was right. That I found out about Chas's theft, at least. Though, contrary to Alison's assumptions, I'd had no intention of making that information public. Not everyone was a blackmailer.

Or killer, I thought, realizing Alison's patience was wearing thin as she took another step toward me.

I tried to take one backwards, but I was pinned against the car.

"And now, you need to go," Alison told me.

That panic in my chest turned into full-blown fear, adrenaline coursing through my veins like fire.

No weapons. No backup. I was on my own. And it was now or never.

I took a deep breath, sucking in courage I wasn't sure I had. "There's just one thing you didn't count on," I told her, false bravado filling my voice.

She frowned. "What, pray tell, is that?"

"That!" I shouted, pointing to the empty field behind her.

On instinct, she turned to look.

Which was exactly what I'd been hoping she'd do. I took her split second of inattention and leapt forward, shoving my right shoulder into her with all my might.

She cried out, falling backward, her hands going behind her to catch her fall.

But I didn't stick around to see if she was okay, taking off at a dead sprint in the other direction, hoping I could dissolve into the darkness before Alison was able to regain her footing. Or aim.

My feet pounded on the hard ground, arms pumping. I felt brambles and vines scrape at my arms and face, but I didn't stop, running blindly. I followed the straight row to the end of the field, only then zigzagging into another row. I had no idea where I was going or how long it would be before I saw something resembling civilization and safety, but I kept running.

I vaguely heard the sound of a car behind me and had the sudden horrible vision of Alison Price mowing me down in a vineyard, taking out an entire crop of Chardonnay grapes along with me. I resisted the urge to stop, turn around, and see how close she was. I knew every second counted, and I needed to keep moving.

While I wasn't exactly a couch potato, I wasn't in marathon shape either. My thighs burned, and my calves threatened to cramp up. My head pounded with each step I took, the ache wearing on me. I pushed harder, pumping my arms for all they were worth, knowing I was on borrowed time. I couldn't run forever. And sooner or later, that car motor I could hear in the distance would catch up to me.

As if on cue, the sounds of gunfire cracked through the night.

I ducked instinctively, though I had no idea if the bullet came anywhere near me. I couldn't see the direction it had come from. I heard the car now idling, and I knew she was out there. How close? That was anyone's guess.

I felt like my lungs were on fire when I finally saw a break in the fields ahead. Lights appeared and disappeared behind a row of tall trees. Headlights.

A road.

I pushed forward with a final sprint of energy, practically throwing myself through the grove of trees as I heard another shot—this time unmistakably closer.

I still wasn't sure where I was, but headlights came toward me on a paved road. I waved my arms in front of me like a mad woman, hailing the driver.

At first I almost thought he didn't see me and would plow me down. But at the last second, he swerved right, pulling up against the embankment. His drivers' side window rolled down, and he leaned an elbow out.

"You okay, miss?" a guy in a trucker hat asked.

I could have kissed him. "Call…9-1-1," I panted.

As his hands reached for his cell, my legs collapsed, the relief too great for them to hold me upright anymore.

CHAPTER TWENTY-ONE

The next hour went by in a blur of police arriving, taking statement after statement, paramedics being called to check on my latest head wound, and the dazed driver of the pickup that had been my knight in rusted armor telling the police that I "Just came from nowhere. All crazed and such."

Alison Price was nowhere to be seen by then, but I was sure she couldn't go far. She was a Price. It wasn't like they just blended in.

I was giving my statement to another uniformed officer for the third time, when I spied a familiar face making his way through the growing crowd of law enforcement and emergency personnel.

Grant.

A lesser woman would have thrown herself into his strong arms the moment he was in sight. Me? I waited until he was standing right in front of me to collapse into his open embrace.

His broad shoulders pillowed my face as all those tears of fear, regret, anger, and pure exhaustion I'd been holding back poured out in the safety of his flannel shirt. In that moment, I felt as if his arms could hold me up against any storm—or crazy baby boomer with a gun. I never wanted him to let me go, but eventually he must have felt the wet spot I was making on his shoulder, and he leaned me back to look at my face.

"Are you okay?" he asked, his voice so soft it was almost a whisper. The enticing intimacy of it sent shivers down my spine.

I nodded, not sure I trusted my voice.

"I mean, really okay?" he pressed, his eyes intent.

I stopped nodding. And shook my head.

"Oh, Emmy." He pulled me in for another fierce hug.

A girl could get used to this.

"What happened?" he finally asked.

I pulled back, took a fortifying breath, and told him about the whole scary ordeal, from the bash on the head to the trunk to Alison's confessions. His face was hard and unreadable the entire time, giving away nothing of his emotion or any hint at how much of Alison's guilt he'd already known about.

When I finally finished the story with my trucker savior, Grant asked, "And you knew all along that she was behind Chas's death?"

"Not really," I confessed. "I mean, some of it I had worked out. Like the poker games and the embezzling. But I was as surprised as you were to find out she was Chas's killer."

He stared at me, his expression unreadable. And it dawned on me.

"You aren't surprised, are you?"

He let out a deep sigh. "Not entirely. We traced the attack on you the other night back to Brackston. Forensics was able to lift a partial latent fingerprint from the rock he used. We were questioning him during the memorial, and while he hadn't broken down yet, I had a feeling that someone in the Price-Pennington household had put him up to it."

"I thought it was David," I told him sheepishly.

"Truth?"

I nodded.

"I did too for awhile."

"So he really is innocent?"

Grant nodded. "At least of this. Cheating at poker? That might be another issue, but I'll leave that to vice if they want to pursue the illegal poker games."

"Will they?" I asked, feeling a bit stronger talking it all out with Grant.

"Doubtful. Too many powerful people were at those games. My best guess? It will all be swept under the rug."

I nodded. I supposed I shouldn't be surprised. And really, it paled in comparison with murder.

"Can I take you home?" Grant asked.

I sent him a smile, the first genuine one I'd felt in what seemed like forever. "I thought you'd never ask."

* * *

Grant dropped me off at my cottage, making sure I made it inside the door before being a gentleman and promising to check in on me the following day. I gratefully collapsed onto my bed, falling asleep fully clothed and not waking again until the sun was high above the horizon. I moved slowly, every limb in my body feeling sore and overexerted. I took the hottest shower known to woman, and dressed in a pair of comfortable pink sweats and an old T-shirt with a picture of Mickey Mouse on it. I checked my phone and saw I had two messages from Grant already. That put a little smile on my face as I made my way toward the scent of coffee in the kitchen.

I spent the rest of the morning simultaneously being fed, coddled, and interrogated by Conchita and Hector about the events of the previous evening. By noon, Ava got in on the action, pulling up in her convertible just as I was considering getting to work. Somehow she convinced me that a bottle of Australian Shiraz and a pint of mint chip were a better idea, and we spent the rest of the afternoon on my sofa, with Thelma, Louise, and Bridget Jones, being grateful for the little things like good wine, chocolate ice cream, and best friends.

* * *

It was the following Friday, and Gene Schulz was smiling as he stood in my office. I could hardly believe what he was telling me, and his seesaw hands were held dead level. Well, almost level. They still tilted a little in the downward direction, but as he beamed about the good press Alison Price's arrest had gotten and how happy his investors were to be backing the "Heroine of Wine Country" who had "single-handedly (at least according to Bradley Wu) caught a killer," his mega-white smile didn't falter a beat.

According to the latest article in the *Sonoma Index-Tribune*, the police had caught up to Alison at the airport, as she'd tried to charter a private plane to Oaxaca, Mexico. Luckily Alison had still been driving Conchita's car, which was thankfully returned to her unharmed. While Alison had vehemently denied any wrongdoing at first, the papers were reporting that they expected her lawyer to put in an insanity plea. I had to agree—that woman was off her rocker.

Vivienne Price-Pennington had declined any comments to the press about the entire affair, quickly leaving the country for Belize, ostensibly to spread Chas's ashes. But I'd heard from Ava, who'd heard it from her father's cleaning lady, that the Price-Pennington estate had been closed up indefinitely. Valuables had been sent to storage, the furniture covered in thick, white sheets, and the staff let go. It didn't appear as if Vivienne had any intention of returning. I didn't blame her. The hodgepodge style mansion on the hill probably held too many bad memories.

According to Schultz, despite her mother's guilt, Vivienne was still the one footing the bill for Alison's very expensive defense attorney. I could only imagine how conflicted Vivienne's feelings must be toward the woman who doted on her, being that she'd also been the one to kill the love of her life. I had no idea if she'd spoken to Alison, but she was fulfilling her daughterly duty from afar.

Vivienne had scarcely been gone a day before Sadie had assumed the role of CEO at Price Digital. Apparently unaffected by the entire situation, Sadie had made lemon-tinis out of lemons, promising to restructure the entire accounting procedures and seemingly covering any misdeeds by Chas in the process—either knowingly or unknowingly. While Sadie might not be shedding a tear of grief over Chas's demise, it looked as though she knew as well as Vivienne that a scandal would only hurt the company—which she still had eyes on taking over.

After being officially cleared of any wrongdoing and having all charges against her dropped, Jenny had decided to move back to Arizona with her parents for a fresh start. As it turned out, Chas's estate had consisted mostly of the jewelry and gifts he'd accumulated from Vivienne, all of his liquid assets having previously gone to pay off his debts. The last of which Jenny took care of by handing the keys to Chas's bright yellow

Lamborghini over to Fast Money Trask. She said Trask was so delighted at having the debt repaid, he even gave Jenny a good deal on selling Chas's Rolex, along with some other jewelry and valuables, in his pawn shop. At least good enough that Jenny said she had enough to build a new life for herself in Arizona, where she could be close to her remaining family.

The only member of the Price-Pennington family who'd stayed out of the media was the brooding artist David Allen. Though, Ava and I had both attended his show at the Salavence Gallery, where he'd sold several pieces. Turned out the Sonoma art lovers were more into dark and angtsy than I'd expected. At the opening, he'd told us he intended to stick around Sonoma for a bit longer, despite his family's tainted reputation. Whether that was a promise, threat, or just casual conversation, I still wasn't sure. While David's poker skills and financial demands on his stepfather had certainly contributed to Chas's demise, I was still adjusting to thinking of him as innocent.

"So, let's talk real numbers, Emmy," Schultz prompted when he'd finished regaling me with media's glowing new take on our winery. "Tell me the bookings have started rolling back in."

I bit my lip. "Do you want me to lie?"

His smile faltered for a second, but it was quickly back as he waved his hands in the air. "Never mind. I'm sure they're on their way. The court of public opinion has proven you innocent, and that's all that matters. You'll soon be in the pink."

I'd be happy just to be in the black. "So you think we'll be able to secure financing for the harvest this year?"

Schultz nodded vigorously. "Sure, sure. Those sales forecasts are about to turn up. I'm positive that by the time you need funding, they'll look healthy enough to woo investors."

I liked his optimism. Even if I knew it was my hard work in the meantime that would make or break that forecast.

As soon as Schultz left, still with a smile and a little spring in his step, I got to work planning a new event—the re-re-launch of the Oak Valley Vineyards. This time it would be a small tasting and dessert to follow. I wanted to let the wine shine through and let the guests enjoy the elegant simplicity of our gorgeous venue. No large meal. No over-the-top preparations. And most importantly, no dead VIPs.

An hour later I was working my way through the guest list, and mentally planning the menu of sweet treats, when a knock sounded at my office door.

"Come in," I answered automatically, halfway hoping it was Conchita with an early dinner delivery.

But the frame that filled the doorway was not that of my pleasantly plump mother figure, but the broad shoulders of Detective Christopher Grant.

"Detective Grant." Caught off guard, I stood up, bumping my knee on the desk in the process. I cringed, resisting the urge to fix my hair as his assessing eyes slid over me.

"You okay?" He gestured to my knee.

"Yes. Fine. Good. Great, even." I cleared the nerves out of my throat.

His eyes crinkled a little at the corners. "Good. I'm glad you're settling back in after everything."

I spread my hands to encompass the mess of spreadsheets, menus, and hastily scrawled lists of VIP names. "Super settled."

"Good." He paused. "Unfortunately, this isn't a social call. I, uh, just stopped by because I wanted to tell you personally before you heard from anyone else. Brackston has accepted a plea deal."

I felt a frown pulling at my forehead. Brackston, the Lurch look-alike butler who'd been arrested for assault and conspiracy. "What sort of deal?"

"He's agreed to flip on Alison Price in exchange for a lesser sentence."

My frown deepened. "How much lesser?"

Grant's turn to clear his throat. In fact, he looked even more uncomfortable than his sudden appearance in my office had made me a moment ago. "A lot lesser. Community service and probation on the assault charges."

"So he's going to walk free for bashing me over the head?" I asked, hearing my voice rise in both volume and pitch.

Grant nodded, his eyes softer as they searched mine. "I'm afraid so."

I breathed in deeply, trying not to freak out as I took mental stock of my feelings on the subject. Let's just say, they weren't warm and fuzzy. The idea of Lurch running around free to bash again left me angry, unsatisfied, and just a little frightened. On the other hand, Alison had committed a far worse sin. I could only imagine what kind of leverage she'd used against Lurch to convince him to do her dirty work. So, while I wasn't thrilled with the outcome, it could have been far worse. At least Alison Price would be locked away, likely for the rest of her life.

"I guess that's okay," I finally decided.

Grant's right eyebrow rose in mild surprise. "It is?"

I shrugged. "I'm not dancing a jig over it, but if that's the best we can do, it could be worse. I mean, I'm alive, right?" And the bruising was even going down to minimally noticeable at this point.

Grant's lips lifted in a smile. "You are." He took a step forward. "And you can be sure I won't let Brackston within a hot mile of the winery again."

The protective note in his voice sent warmth spreading through my belly. "Thanks. I appreciate that."

"You're welcome." He paused again. "But you know what I'd appreciate?" he asked, taking another step closer. So close I could almost reach out and touch him.

I licked my lips. "Yes?"

"A glass of that Petite Sirah I've heard so much about." He punctuated the request with a wink.

Was Grant flirting with me? The little gold flecks in his amber eyes moved in a mischievous dance, his smile curved in a wicked tilt, and he was still standing close enough to me that I could smell the faint aroma of his aftershave—something woodsy and fresh. I tried not to inhale too deeply, lest I lose my hold on long dormant hormones that were suddenly waking with a vengeance.

"You mean, you'd dare to try my 'killer wine'?" I teased back.

His eyes twinkled at me. "What can I say? I like to live dangerously."

"I'll say. Drinking on duty?"

"I'm actually off duty today."

I raised one eyebrow his way. "Really? So this *is* a social call?"

He chuckled, the sound a warm rumble that I swore I could almost feel vibrating through my belly. "I suppose it is," he replied. "Do you mind?"

Mind? My head was suddenly racing with all sorts of implications in that one statement. Most of them ending completely scandalously. "I don't think I do mind," I told him truthfully.

"Then lead the way, Ms. Oak." He stepped back to allow me to pass by him, his hand going ever so lightly to the small of my back as I did.

I stifled a shiver.

"Just one thing though, Detective Grant," I told him as we headed toward the tasting room.

"Yes?"

"If we're going to be on social terms, call me Emmy."

He came up beside me. *Close* beside me. His eyes were dark, his voice low and intimate. "With pleasure," he promised.

My stomach instantly turned to jelly. That was it. Grant was definitely trouble with a capital *T*.

And the worst thing about it?

I kinda liked it.

RECIPES

Emmy's Spanish Style Paella

2 tablespoons olive oil
1 tablespoon sweet or smoked paprika
2 teaspoons oregano
salt and pepper to taste
1 frying chicken, cut into pieces (roughly 3 lbs.)
1/4 cup extra-virgin olive oil
2 Spanish chorizo sausages, thickly sliced
1 onion, diced
1 red bell pepper, finely chopped
2 cloves of crushed garlic
1 bunch flat-leaf parsley leaves, chopped, reserve some for garnish
1 (15 oz) can diced or crushed tomatoes, drained
4 cups short grain Spanish rice
6 cups water, warm
generous pinch of saffron threads
8 mussels, scrubbed
1/2 pound jumbo shrimp, peeled and deveined
1/2 cup frozen peas
lemon wedges, for serving

In a medium bowl, combine the paprika, oregano, the 2 tablespoons of olive oil, and salt and pepper, and coat the chicken in the mixture. Then marinate the chicken in the refrigerator. (This can be done up to a day ahead.)

Heat the olive oil in a large pan or paella pan over medium-high heat. Sauté the chorizo until browned, then remove and set aside. Heat the shrimp for roughly 2 minutes, until pink, and set aside. Cook the chicken, skin-side down, until browned on all sides. While cooking, season with more salt and pepper. When browned, remove from pan and set aside.

In the same pan, prepare the sofrito. Sauté the onions, red pepper, and parsley until onions begin to get soft, about 3 minutes. Add tomatoes and cook until the mixture begins to caramelize and thicken a bit. Then add in the rice, coating all of the grains in the tomato mixture. Add in water, chicken, sausage, and saffron, and bring to a simmer for about 10 minutes, stirring frequently so the rice cooks evenly. Add mussels to pan, nestling them into rice mixture. Cook about 5 minutes or until the shells open. Nestle the shrimp into the rice mixture and add the frozen peas. Cook about 5–10 minutes or until shrimp are done and rice is cooked.

When the rice looks fluffy and moist, turn the heat up for just a few seconds until you can smell the rice toasting (but not burning) at the bottom of the pan. This is called the *socarrat.*

Remove from heat and garnish with lemon wedges and additional parsley.

While Emmy was cooking this in bulk for her Spanish event, this recipe serves 8.

Shortcuts!
If you want a simpler version to make at home, you can use boneless, skinless chicken breast and purchase your shrimp already peeled and deveined. Clams can be substituted for mussels—you can even use canned ones. You can cook the chorizo, chicken (cut into bit-sized pieces), and shrimp all in the same pan together—adding the chicken first, then chorizo, and finally shrimp, which takes the least time to cook. Use Minute Rice to cut down on cooking time!

Wine Pairings
Best served paired with chilled, fruity wines, like a rosé or Sauvignon Blanc, or a chilled sangria like the one Emmy prepared. Some of Emmy's other suggestions: Kendall-Jackson Vintner's Reserve Rosé, Chateau d'Esclans Côtes de Provence Whispering Angel Rosé, Sterling Sauvignon Blanc Napa.

Baked Brie Fettuccini

8 oz brie
1/2 lb. fettuccini noodles
2 teaspoons extra-virgin olive oil
1/4 cup onion, chopped
2 strips of bacon, chopped
1 clove garlic, minced
2 tablespoons chopped parsley
red pepper flakes to taste
salt to taste
1/4 cup grated Parmesan cheese

Cut the rind off the brie, then put it in a skillet or baking pan. Bake in the oven at 350°F until the brie is melted and bubbling, roughly 10–15 minutes.

While the brie is melting, cook the fettuccini noodles in a large pot of boiling salted water. When slightly al dente, drain the pasta and reserve some of the cooking liquid.
In a medium pan, heat the olive oil, garlic, onion, and bacon. Cook until the bacon is crispy and the onion is translucent.

Toss the cooked fettuccini with the bacon, garlic, onion mixture. Add the fresh chopped parsley and red pepper flakes.
Once the brie is done, remove from the oven and immediately add the fettuccini to it, using tongs to coat. If the brie is too thick, you can add a little of the pasta water to thin it to a nice saucy consistency. Top with grated parmesan and enjoy!

Serves two hungry people.

Wine Pairings
Best served paired with a fruity red, like a Pinot Noir, or creamy white wine, like a Chardonnay. Some of Emmy's suggestions: Dark Horse Rosé, Mumm Napa Blanc de Blancs Champagne, Heron Chardonnay, Amici Chardonnay Sonoma Coast.

Espresso Waffles with Mocha Sauce

1 cup sweetened condensed milk
1/4 cup strong coffee
4 oz dark chocolate, finely chopped
1 cup all-purpose flour
1/4 cup cocoa powder
1 tablespoon espresso powder
1 teaspoon baking powder
1 teaspoon baking soda
1 tablespoon sugar
1/2 teaspoon salt
1 cup whole milk
2 tablespoons melted butter
3 eggs
toasted almond slivers for garnish
fresh raspberries for garnish

Over medium heat, combine in a saucepan the sweetened condensed milk and coffee. Bring it to a boil, stirring constantly to avoid the milk burning. Remove from the heat and add the chocolate. Whisk it until smooth and keep warm, but not hot.

In a large mixing bowl, whisk flour, cocoa powder, espresso powder, baking powder, baking soda, sugar, and salt. In a smaller bowl, mix together the milk with the melted butter and eggs until smooth. Add to the dry ingredients and stir just until combined—do not over stir.

Bake in a waffle iron according the manufacturer's directions until crisp on the edges.

Drizzle each waffle with some of the mocha sauce, and garnish with the almonds and raspberries. Enjoy!

This recipe makes about 6 waffles, depending on size.

Shortcuts!

You can use waffle or pancake mix, and just add in the espresso powder and cocoa powder before mixing according to the package directions.

Beverage Pairings
Pair with a warm latte or Raspberry Bellinis (recipe below!).

Raspberry Bellinis

1/2 cup raspberries (fresh or frozen and thawed)
1 tablespoon sugar
1 (750-ml) bottle chilled champagne, prosecco, or other sparkling wine

In a small bowl, mash the raspberries with the sugar until the sugar is dissolved and mixture is smooth. Put about a tablespoon of the puree into a champagne flute. Then slowly fill with champagne, being careful, as it will fizz. Repeat for the other glasses.

Makes 4 delightful breakfast cocktails

Mexican Lasagna

1 lb. ground pork
2 tablespoons olive oil
1/2 small red onion, chopped
1 green pepper, chopped
1 red pepper, chopped
2 teaspoons smoked paprika
1 teaspoon cumin
1 tablespoon chili powder
1 teaspoon salt
1 (14.5 oz) can diced fire-roasted tomatoes
1 cup frozen corn
1 (10 oz) can enchilada sauce
12 large 8" flour or corn tortillas
16 oz shredded Mexican cheese blend (Monterey Jack and cheddar)
1 (6 oz) can sliced olives
2 tablespoons cilantro, chopped

Preheat your oven to 425°F.

Heat olive oil in a large skillet over medium heat. Add ground pork, onion, peppers, paprika, cumin, chili powder, and salt. Cook for about 10 minutes, until the pork is browned and the onions and peppers are soft. Add the tomatoes and corn and stir to combine the ingredients. Keep warm on low heat.

Add about 1/3 of the enchilada sauce to the bottom of a 9x13 baking pan. Grab 4 tortillas: keep 2 whole, cut 1 in half, and cut 1 in fourths. Lay the two whole tortillas on the bottom of the pan, put the 4 quartered tortillas in the corners (right angles facing the corners), and lay the 2 halved tortillas on the rectangular sides (cut side at the edge of the pan). This should totally cover the bottom of the pan.

Spoon half of the pork mixture over top of the tortillas and spread evenly. Create another tortilla layer on top of this and drizzle another 1/3 of the enchilada sauce over the tortillas. Sprinkle 1/2 of the cheese over this, then add the rest of the pork mixture. Create one more tortilla layer on top of the pork, then drizzle the remaining enchilada sauce over tortillas. Sprinkle remaining cheese on top of tortillas and scatter the olive slices on top.

Bake for about 15 minutes, or until the cheese is melted and the sauce is bubbly. Remove from oven and garnish with fresh cilantro. Enjoy!

(Some other optional but tasty garnishes are guacamole and sour cream!)

Shortcuts!
You can use taco seasoning instead of the spices in the pork mixture and substitute canned green chilies instead of the chopped red and green pepper. Buying pre-shredded Mexican cheese blend is a time saver too! Don't have enchilada sauce on hand? You can substitute salsa.

Wine Pairings
While Mexican food is usually served with beer, there are several wines that complement the spicy, rich flavors. Try pairing with crisp whites, like a Sauvignon Blanc or Pinot Grigio, or fruity reds, like a Zinfandel or Pinot Noir. Some of Emmy's suggestions: Beringer Zinfandel, Chateau St. Jean Sauvignon Blanc, Decoy Sonoma County Pinot Noir.

Truffle Risotto Bites

Risotto is made out of arborio rice, an Italian short-grain rice. When cooking the arborio over low heat and adding liquid, the short grains will absorb the liquid and release starch at the same time, resulting in an ultra creamy risotto.

8 cups chicken broth (or for a vegetarian dish, use vegetable broth!)
1/2 onion, minced
4 tablespoons butter
2 cups arborio rice
3/4 cup dry white wine
1/2 cup finely grated parmesan cheese
2 tablespoons white truffle oil
1/2 teaspoon salt
1 cup breadcrumbs
vegetable oil for frying

Heat the broth in a medium saucepan until hot but not boiling. Keep hot on the stove.

In a large pan, melt 2 tablespoons of butter and sauté onions until translucent. Add the rice and stir continuously for about a minute until all the rice is coated with the butter. Add the wine and stir continuously again until the wine is absorbed into the rice—about 2 minutes. Then add about 1 cup (or 1 ladle full) of the hot broth to the rice and stir continuously until the broth is almost absorbed into the rice. Add the rest of the broth the same way, 1 cup at a time, until the rice is tender and mixture is creamy—about 25–30 minutes.

Reduce heat to low and stir in parmesan cheese, truffle oil, last 2 tablespoons of butter, and salt to taste.

Refrigerate the mixture until chilled, roughly an hour.

Roll the risotto mixture into 1 inch balls. If too sticky to easily handle, coat your fingers with cold water first. Then coat balls in breadcrumbs.

You can either drop the balls into a deep fryer or fry on the stove in oil, turning occasionally until all sides are browned. Once browned, set balls on a paper towel to absorb excess oil. Enjoy!

Makes about 24 Risotto Bites.

Shortcuts!
If you're not a risotto purist, you can use a time-saver shortcut. Instead of arborio rice, use Minute Rice. If truffle oil isn't readily available, you can add finely chopped sautéed mushrooms for a similar earthly flavor that will complement the parmesan cheese.

Wine Pairings
Best served with bold white wines, like a lightly oaked Chardonnay. Some of Emmy's suggestions: Woodbridge Lightly Oaked Chardonnay, Chateau Ste. Michelle Chardonnay Canoe Ridge, Rombauer Chardonnay Carneros.

ABOUT THE AUTHOR

Gemma Halliday is the #1 Amazon, *New York Times & USA Today* bestselling author of several mystery series. Gemma's books have received numerous awards, including a Golden Heart, two National Reader's Choice awards, three RITA nominations, a RONE award for best mystery, and two Killer Nashville Silver Flachion Awards for best cozy mystery and readers' choice. She currently lives in the San Francisco Bay Area with her large, loud, and loving family.

To learn more about Gemma, visit her online at www.GemmaHalliday.com

Other series in print now from Gemma Halliday...

www.GemmaHalliday.com